**The darkness. The tunnel.
The hospital room. An older couple
who said they loved her and
prayed for her.
None of it made any sense.**

Slightly turning her head, Tavia peered into the face of yet another stranger. A handsome man in a wheelchair with a small vase of white daisies balanced between his knees.

"Hi. They said you were awake. I've been so worried about you." He placed the vase on the nightstand. "I want you to know how sorry I am. If it weren't for me, you wouldn't have been injured. I did everything I could to avoid the accident, but there wasn't anything I could do."

Accident. This must be the man she heard earlier. Beck. She tried to speak, but the tubes prevented her.

"I shouldn't have mentioned that. I didn't mean to upset you—I'll leave now."

Bewildered, Tavia watched him go. All her life no one had cared if she lived or died; now three strangers were concerned about her.

JOYCE LIVINGSTON

is a Kansan who has held many dream jobs, from being a television broadcaster of eighteen years, to owning her own retail clothing store, to lecturing on quilting and sewing, to writing magazine articles, to being a part-time tour escort, to having over twenty inspirational romance novels contracted, eleven already published. Her books have won numerous awards: Favorite Contemporary Book of both 2000 and 2002, and in 2003 she was named Author of the Year. Her lifetime dream came true last fall when she got word from her agent that Love Inspired wanted to buy this book, *The Heart's Choice*.

THE HEART'S CHOICE

JOYCE LIVINGSTON

Steeple
Hill®

Published by Steeple Hill Books™

STEEPLE HILL BOOKS

Steeple
Hill®

ISBN 0-373-87300-X

THE HEART'S CHOICE

www.SteepleHill.com

Printed in U.S.A.

Behold, I have graven thee upon the palms of
my hands; thy walls are continually before me.
—*Isaiah* 49:16

Oh, my, where do I start?
I owe so much to so many.

Family, friends, other authors. My editor,
Krista Stroever, who really knows her stuff.
My hands-on agent, Carolyn Grayson, who has
great confidence in me and continually spurs me
on. And most of all, my husband, Don, for being
so supportive of my writing, loving leftovers and
putting up with all my idiosyncrasies. I also owe a
debt of gratitude to Tracie Peterson, who has been
a real mentor to me and taught me much about
writing, and to Rebecca Germany for taking that
first chance on me and publishing my first book.

Then, there is Morgan Chilson, who so capably
copyedits for me, and Jean Buchanan, who
volunteers to be my reader. And I can't leave
out my writing group, the wonderful
Kansas Fiction Writers.

But, in addition to the above, I want to acknowledge
you—the reader who has purchased this book.
I hope you enjoy *The Heart's Choice*, my first
book for Love Inspired. I loved writing it,
and hope to write many more Love Inspired
books to share with you in the future.

Chapter One

The woman in the passenger seat quickly rolled down the window as the SUV careened to a stop, its tires making a crunching sound as they left the Colorado highway and rolled onto the uneven shoulder. "What's the problem?" she called out to Tavia, who was standing at the edge of the road, dressed in jeans and a short-sleeved print top, both insufficient to ward off the chill of the late afternoon.

Tavia MacRae blinked hard and tried to appear calm, although inside she was a jangle of nerves. "My—my new boyfriend dumped me out of his car. I—I need a ride."

The nice-looking young man behind the steering wheel frowned as he sized her up from head to toe. "I don't know. I usually don't pick up strangers."

Disappointed by his comment and afraid her boyfriend might return, Tavia allowed her jaw to drop. "Then why did you stop?"

"I asked him to." The pretty brunette in the front seat gave her a warm smile. "You looked like you needed help."

"His hands were all over me. He tried—" Tavia dipped her head and swallowed hard but couldn't hold back a sob as the tip of her finger touched her swollen lip. "Wh-when I wouldn't—you know—he got really mad and started pushing me around and hitting me with his fists. I—I was afraid he was really going to hurt me, but instead he reached across and opened the door and shoved me out." She hunched her shoulders and shivered as she rubbed at her skinned elbow. "He wouldn't even let me have my jacket. He—he just drove off and left me here."

The man raised a brow. "He was your boyfriend?"

Tavia shook her head. Her lip hurt, and so did her arm and her wrist. But what hurt most was the embarrassment she felt at having to admit she'd been so gullible. "He wasn't really my boyfriend. This—this was the first time I'd been out with him. He—he seemed real nice when I met him."

The woman winced at Tavia's words. "Maybe you should have gotten to know him better before deciding to take such a long ride with him."

Tavia lowered her eyes, knowing the woman was right. "I don't have the opportunity to meet men that often. I guess I was persuaded by his good looks and his nice car. I've learned my lesson."

The man continued to eye her suspiciously, as if he

half believed her story but wasn't quite sure she could be trusted. "I don't know. Maybe it—"

The nice brunette slapped at the man's arm. "Adam, come on. Don't be such an old worrywart. Can't you see she needs help? We can't leave her stranded out here on the road. The sun will be disappearing behind the mountains any time now and she'll freeze in that lightweight shirt. She's already shivering. At least let her use your cell phone so she can call someone."

Tavia waited, too humiliated to meet his gaze, her heart pounding in her throat, knowing there was no one she could call, and who knew when someone else would come by and give her a ride? Maybe it would be someone even more dangerous than the man who'd dumped her. Why did she always pick the losers? If she'd been smarter, been a little more cautious—

Frowning, the man handed Tavia his cell phone. She punched in a few random numbers then, after turning away from them, pressed the End button and pretended to be waiting for someone to answer. "Uh-oh. Looks like they're not home and I don't know anyone else who would be willing to drive this far to pick me up. Are you sure you can't give me a ride?"

The woman leaned toward him. "Adam, please?"

He took a deep breath and let it out slowly, his arms circling the steering wheel as he turned toward the open window and hitched his head toward the back seat. "Okay, climb in, but we're only taking you as far as the next town." He paused long enough to give her a warning frown. "You understand?"

Tavia yanked open the back door of the big, shiny SUV when she heard the lock click open and climbed in, closing it quickly behind her before they had a chance to change their minds. "I can't begin to tell you how much I appreciate this. It seems like I've been standing on this road for hours. The traffic has been whizzing by me and no one would stop."

"They probably had better sense than I did," the man said gruffly, his eyes trained on the rear-view mirror as he cautiously pulled back onto the highway.

The woman sitting beside him leaned into his shoulder and smiled up at him. "Now, sweetie, don't be such an old bear. I respect this woman for refusing that man and fighting him off like she did. You should, too."

He seemed to deliberate her words carefully; finally glancing back over his shoulder at Tavia with a nod and, for the first time, offering a half smile. "Sorry. She's right. It's just that you can't be too careful these days."

"Thanks, I don't blame you for being cautious." Tavia leaned back in the seat and tried to calm down. Every bone in her body ached. "I wouldn't pick up a hitch-hiker, either."

"But you're not a hitchhiker," the woman refuted adamantly. "You're someone in trouble. To me, there's a big difference."

Tavia smiled appreciatively, sure if it hadn't been

for the nice woman's influence on the man she assumed was her husband, she'd still be standing by the side of the road. "Thanks. It's nice to have someone who understands."

The woman shifted her position and extended her hand over the back of her seat. "Hi. I'm Jewel Mallory."

"Hi, Jewel. I'm Tavia."

"Tavia? What a pretty name. I've never heard it before."

Tavia smoothed at the tear on her shirt. "Thanks. I think it's Scottish. I like your name, too. It sounds real elegant."

"That's what I keep telling her," Adam inserted, smiling at the lovely lady seated beside him. "She's my jewel. I told my folks, she's not only a jewel, she has a heart of pure gold. But then, I guess you've realized that."

Jewel gave him another playful pat. "Why, Adam, what a sweet thing to say."

He grinned. "Simply the truth, my precious."

Jewel's hand cradled the man's shoulder. "Well, Tavia, this man, who appears to be my biggest fan, is my fiancé, Adam Flint."

"You're engaged?" Tavia looked from one smiling face to the other. "Congratulations. When are you getting married? Have you set a date yet?"

"In the spring, right after I graduate," the man chimed in, his smile broadening, his sullen behavior suddenly changing for the better. "I'm taking Jewel home to meet my parents."

Tavia's brows lifted in surprise. "They haven't already met her?"

Adam shot a quick glance toward his intended. "Not yet, but they've talked to her on the phone a number of times. We met in California where I've been going to school. She's originally from Tennessee."

"But they have seen your picture, right?" Tavia asked.

"I take terrible pictures." Jewel's hand went to her mouth to stifle a giggle. "I hate having my picture taken and I guess it shows on my face. I end up looking like a mug shot for the post-office wall. I wouldn't let Adam send them any."

Adam gave his fiancée a wink. "She's not kidding. As much as I love her, she's not at all photogenic."

"He's right. That's exactly what my mom used to say when I'd bring those school pictures home."

"Besides, I want them to be surprised by her inner beauty, as well." Adam sent a man-in-love look toward his beloved. "Once they meet her, I know they'll fall in love with her instantly, just like I did."

Jewel smiled shyly. "Don't listen to him, Tavia. He's a real flatterer, but I love every minute of it."

Adam glanced in his side mirror before continuing. "We talked about getting married earlier, but my parents want to throw us a big spring wedding."

Tavia frowned. "You mean you're not living together?"

"We're both kinda old-fashioned, I guess. We're both Christians, and didn't feel it was right to just move in together like many of our friends have done. In fact, we've even had separate motel rooms on our trip here."

"I'm sure your parents are happy about that."

"Oh, yes," Adam volunteered, catching her eye in the rearview mirror. "But they're a pretty romantic pair themselves, even after being together nearly twenty-eight years."

Tavia wished she had someone who loved her as much as Adam appeared to love Jewel. His devotion for her was written all over his smiling face.

Jewel reached across and cupped Adam's cheek with her palm, her hand caressing his face. "Although we really wanted to get married right away, we talked it over and decided since we are committing our lives to each other and this was going to be our one and only wedding, we wanted to do it up right."

Tavia eyed the woman suspiciously. "You're not—"

"Pregnant? Oh, my, no!" Jewel gave her head a firm shake. "But we do plan to have children—someday. Adam's parents have his little baby bed stored in their attic, along with his high chair and his stroller. Our children might use the very same things their father used when he was a baby. Won't that be sweet?"

"Hopefully, we can start a family a year or so after I graduate," Adam added.

"I hope so, too." Jewel pinched Adam's arm affectionately. "From what Adam's parents have told me on the phone, they want to invite all theirs and Adam's friends and business acquaintances to our wedding. Do the big church thing, with the huge reception. His mother and I are going to have a blast planning it."

Adam gave her a quick sideways look of adoration. It was obvious he was crazy about her.

"How about your parents, Jewel?" Tavia asked. "Are they disappointed you aren't going to have your wedding in Tennessee?" As soon as she spoke, Tavia wished she hadn't asked the woman such a personal question. What business was it of hers?

"Jewel doesn't have any family," Adam answered, even though Tavia's question had been directed toward her. "Her mom and dad were killed in a car wreck when she was a senior in high school. Other than a couple of distant relatives she hasn't heard from in years, she's pretty much alone."

Jewel lowered her head and blinked hard. "It was a terrible time for me. We'd been so close that for a while I wished I were dead, too. I had great parents."

"Having family around you, family who loves you and who you can depend on, must be a wonderful thing. I wish I'd been that lucky." Tavia's heart went out to her.

Jewel's face brightened. "Well, I have a family now. I have Adam and his parents."

"And they're going to love you as much as I do, honey." Adam lifted her hand to his lips and kissed it. "You'll see. Mom's always wanted a daughter. Now she has one."

"I'm so anxious to meet Adam's parents," Jewel said. "I've missed being a part of a family these past three years. Mr. and Mrs. Flint are lovely, caring people. I've received such sweet letters from them, besides talking to them on the phone. They've told me so many cute things about this man I'm going to marry. They even told me about the time he—"

Over Adam's half-joking protestations, Jewel began. "Adam's parents had just moved into their new home and they invited everyone from their church to come to an open house. His mother spent all morning in the kitchen, making her famous cherry chocolate brownies as the main dessert. Just before their guests were due to arrive, she added the final touches to each of her beautiful brownies—a huge dollop of freshly whipped cream and one perfect, maraschino cherry, then carried the huge silver trays into the dining room and placed them on the beautifully set table. She lit the candles, then closed the dining room doors, planning to keep her lovely table and all its goodies out of sight until everyone arrived."

Adam reached across with a good-humored frown and tapped Jewel's shoulder. "Okay, sweetheart, this is your last chance. You'd better quit while you're ahead or I'll tell my story, too."

"Too late, Adam. I've already started my story. I have to finish."

Tavia glanced out the side window. Already, the sun had disappeared behind the mountain range. It was great that this couple had been kind enough to give her a ride, but what was she going to do when they let her out?

"Anyway, when it came time to serve the refreshments, Adam's mother proudly threw open the dining room door—and let out a scream!"

Tavia gasped. "Why? What had happened?"

Jewel let out an animated laugh. "Someone had removed every single cherry and had run a finger through each dollop of whipped cream, stringing it all over the brownies!"

"Not Adam!"

"Yes, Adam. My prim and proper Adam!" Jewel nodded.

Adam gave her a menacing glare, though his eyes showed it was only in jest. "I'll get you for this, Miss Blabbermouth."

"But that's not all," Jewel went on. "In the resultant shocked silence, they heard a terrible moaning and groaning coming from the bathroom at the head of the stairs. Adam's parents rushed up to see what it was, and there was Adam—his little hands resting on the sides of the toilet seat and he was—"

Adam reached across and cupped his palm over Jewel's mouth. "I think she gets the picture, Jewel. You needn't go into any more detail."

Peeking over his hand, Jewel's eyes glittered with amusement. Tavia couldn't contain her laughter. In her mind's eye, she could see the scene Jewel had described.

Finally, Adam took his hand away. "Sorry, Tavia, sometimes my fiancée is a bit over the top."

"Okay, you win, Adam," Jewel said, smiling at him, "I won't give her all the gory details, but I will tell her to this day you refuse maraschino cherries and whipped cream. On anything!"

Adam glanced at Tavia in the rearview mirror. "My turn now."

"Don't believe a word he says, Tavia," Jewel cautioned, patting her fiancé's cheek. "He has a tendency to exaggerate things."

Adam sent her a good-natured frown. "Me? You're the one who exaggerates."

"I only embellish a good story, dear. There's a difference!"

How Tavia longed to have this kind of relationship with a man, but it never seemed to happen to her. She met few men as warm and friendly as Adam.

"Embellish? That's what you call it?" Adam checked the traffic to his right and changed lanes before going on. "Okay, Tavia. Let me tell you about this woman. She actually stalked me from the first time she saw me."

"I wouldn't exactly call it stalking." Jewel settled herself back into the seat. "But I did think you were adorable, and I wanted to meet you."

"I hate to brag," Adam went on, "but I'm a pretty good ice skater. I've been skating since I was in junior high. Though I didn't skate much during my first three years at college, the apartment I moved into at the end of my junior year was just down the street from a skating rink. I figured, rather than go to the student union and bowl or work out, skating would be a great way to get some exercise, and I started going every Friday and Saturday night. One Friday night, as I was skating along, doing some fancy footwork and minding my own business, this pretty gal skates right across in front of me and falls down!" He gave Jewel a wink. "So? What's a gentleman supposed to do? I stopped to make sure she was okay, then helped her up. She'd skinned her knee a bit, so I took her arm and skated her to the front of the rink and offered to buy her a cup of hot cocoa."

"I took him up on it immediately!"

Tavia had to laugh at the look on Jewel's face as she spoke.

"Anyway," he went on, "after she finished her cocoa, I asked the lady at the concession stand for a little bandage to put on her knee and helped her to where she'd left her jacket and shoes."

"Then what?" This was like a Cinderella story and Tavia was eager to hear the rest.

"I have to admit she was pretty cute, so I hung around until she came back out onto the ice, then asked her to skate with me when the rink's announcer called for a couples-only skate. She hung on to my arm like she was afraid she was going to fall down again, and she kept telling me what a wonderful skater I was."

Tavia clapped her hands. "Oh, that's such a sweet story."

"Hey, that's not all of it. She showed up at the rink again the next night and batted those baby blues at me. Of course, I asked her to skate again, and again she clung tightly to my arm. I figured she must have just started skating and I wanted to do everything I could to help her, so I put my arm around her as we skated, to help steady her. By the end of the evening, she had me under her spell. From that moment on, I never even looked at another girl."

Tavia leaned forward, placing her hand on his shoulder. "That is such a romantic story, Adam. Thank you for telling it to me."

Adam caught her reflection in the mirror. "Hey, there's more."

"There's more?"

"Yes. Six months later, Jewel confessed to me she'd learned to skate when she was in high school! That woman had been stalking me for several weeks, trying to figure out a way to meet me, before she came up with that idea of falling down in front of me! She was nearly as good a skater as me!"

Tavia turned to Jewel and gasped. "You didn't!"

"Oh, but I did, and it worked. Look what happened! I'm engaged to the guy!"

"You are both lucky to have found each other. Adam, I'm sure your parents are going to love Jewel when they finally get to meet her."

"Adam has told me so much about them. I think his mother and I must be a lot alike. Even though Adam and his father hate rhubarb, she's as crazy about it as I am. We both hate scary movies and cry at sad ones and we both love to read in bed. He says his mother always has a stack of romance novels on her nightstand, waiting to be read." Jewel brushed a lock of hair from her face and anchored it behind one ear. "How about your family, Tavia? You said that man back there was your boyfriend. Or should I say a new acquaintance? I guess that means you're not married."

"No, I'm not." Tavia stared out the window, the pain of her past as vivid as if it were yesterday. "I—I don't have a family, either. My mom died of cancer when I was two. I don't remember her at all."

"Your father raised you?"

"My dad drank himself to death when I was seven. I was sent to live with an aunt and uncle I'd never met. They really didn't want me. When I was sixteen, I ran away. I've been on my own ever since. End of sad story."

Jewel's eyes grew round. "And now this has happened to you? You poor thing! And I thought I had it bad, losing my parents like I did."

Adam smiled over the seat at Tavia. "Sorry. I had no

idea what you've gone through. I'm glad we stopped to help you."

"Me, too," Tavia responded, wondering what would have happened to her if this nice couple hadn't come along.

"Adam's going to be a doctor, like his father," Jewel announced proudly, as if wanting to change the subject for their passenger's sake. "Only he's going to be an ob/gyn. His father specializes in dermatology."

"A doctor? That'll be nice," Tavia answered, not exactly sure what an ob/gyn did. She cast an embarrassed glance over her shabby jeans and her simple print shirt—clothes she'd bought at the Goodwill store. Rich parents, a new SUV, beautiful clothes. A good future ahead of them. *This nice couple has it made and what do I have? Nothing. Absolutely nothing but bills I can't pay and a lousy job I'm about to lose.*

Adam flipped on the turn signal and moved back into the inside lane. "I sure hope you'll be able to get someone to come after you soon."

"I hope so, too." Although Tavia was grateful for the ride, she knew she had no choice but to try to hitch another lift into Denver from wherever they'd leave her off. There really wasn't anyone to call. Not anyone she trusted to show up, and she certainly didn't have any money for a motel. The waitress she worked with at the café had three kids to support and didn't even have a car. The woman who lived next door to her was probably too drunk to answer the phone. Her landlord was even less trustworthy than the man who'd let her out on the roadside. Her boss at the video store where she worked part-time was already on the verge of firing her. She'd never call him.

"You do have someone to call, don't you?" Jewel prodded, noticing her hesitation.

"Ah—yeah. I'll just keep calling that woman I tried to reach on your cell phone until she gets home. You can just drop me off anywhere. I'll be fine."

Jewel took off her seat belt to pick up her purse from the floor. She pulled out a ten-dollar bill. "Here, take this. You'll need money for the pay phone and to get a bite to eat while you're waiting."

Tavia ignored her offer and turned her head away. "No, I couldn't. You've already done more for me than most people would."

"I insist."

"Yeah," Adam chimed in, "go ahead and take it. You'll need it."

Tavia was tempted to reach for it. She really did need it, but pulled her hand away. "Only if you'll let me mail it back to you when I get my next paycheck."

Jewel reached the money out to her again. "I have a better idea. Next time you see someone in need, you give them a ten-dollar bill and we'll call it square. Okay? You can even put it in the Salvation Army pot at Christmas if you'd rather."

Tavia stared at the bill. No doubt there would be a long-distance charge if she could figure out someone to call. Smiling, she accepted it, folded it carefully and stuck it into her pocket.

Beck Brewster gave a big yawn as he leaned back in the seat and stretched first one long arm, then the other. He'd been on the road for nearly seven hours now and his back was beginning to feel it. He set the brake on his eighteen-wheeler, grabbed his coffee mug and climbed down from the cab.

Another eighteen-wheeler, much like his, pulled into the Colorado rest-stop parking lot and swung into the stall beside Beck's. The driver gave him a wave, then shoved open his door and dropped down to the pavement. "Hiya, Brewster. Didn't expect to run into you today. How goes it?"

"Hey, yourself, Matt. Where ya headed?"

The man shielded his eyes from the brilliant afternoon sun with one hand. "Littleton. Where you headed?"

Beck pulled a pack of gum from his pocket, took out a stick, and offered the pack to the man. "Headed back to Denver. Hope to drop my load and be in my own bed by ten o'clock tonight. Boy, I hate sleeping in motels. Don't think I'll ever get used to it. Of course, sleeping in the cab is even worse."

"I'm having a bit of trouble with my windshield wipers." Matt shook his head with a laugh as he gestured upward. "But from the looks of that cloudless sky, I don't think it'll be a problem to make it on into Littleton without them."

Beck nodded and glanced skyward. "You're probably right. Sure hope I make it okay."

"Oh? Why?"

Beck placed his mug on the step and began examining the brake lines. "Nothing, I hope. I just have this strange feeling. I hate going through these mountains with a full load. I always worry about the brakes holding. And the noise those Jake brakes make gives me the willies. Guess I'm a natural worrier."

"Bet you carry a rabbit's foot, too."

Beck shook his head. "I didn't say I was superstitious, just a worrier. There's a big difference."

"Well, unfortunately, we have to depend on the guys who do the maintenance on these babies, but they seem to know their job. I sure wouldn't be much help to them. I barely know a flywheel from a crankshaft," Matt said. "I need to hit the walking trail and stretch my legs a bit before I leave. The old bones ain't what they used to be, and I wanna rinse out my mug and get some pop from the pop machine."

Beck gave the man a mock salute. "Then I'll see you around. I'd wait until you're ready to go and follow you on down but I wanna keep on schedule. Drive safe."

"You, too. I'll probably see you next week."

"Yep. Catch you later."

The two men shook hands, then Beck headed off.

"Boy, I hate driving through these mountains."

Jewel smiled at Adam. "I'd offer to drive, but I know he wouldn't let me."

"Hey, even though I've driven this road all my life, I still worry about it."

Jewel poked Adam's ribs playfully. "I don't know why. You're a great driver."

Adam gave her a boyish smile. "Keep that flattery coming!"

"Your ring is beautiful," Tavia told Jewel as the woman relaxed her hand across the seat back. She'd never seen such a beautiful ring, or such large stones.

Jewel's face beamed with pride. "It was Adam's mother's engagement ring. His dad bought her a new set for their twenty-fifth wedding anniversary. So when they learned we were engaged, they wanted me to have her engagement ring."

"We'd planned to come home this past Christmas, but the day we were to leave Jewel came down with the flu and I had to come on and leave her behind. I knew it would kill my folks if I didn't spend Christmas with them. I brought Mom's ring back with me and gave it to her."

"You're so lucky to have found each other," Tavia said sincerely as she looked from one to the other. They were a handsome couple, and it was obvious they adored one another. She'd never had anyone look at her the way Adam looked at Jewel. And she probably never would. The kind of guys she met were definitely not the romantic type. How had she ever let that creep talk her into going for a drive up in the mountains with him? She should've known he'd put the make on her. The crumb-bum. Well, she'd learned her lesson. Next time, she'd be more careful.

Jewel slipped the ring off her finger. "Wanna try it on?"

Tavia stared at her in amazement. "Me? Try on your ring? Goodness, no!"

"Oh, come on. It'll make your hand look really pretty."

Tavia backed away and folded her arms over her chest. "I couldn't. With my luck, I might lose it or something."

"In the car?" Jewel let out a chuckle. "Even if you dropped it, I'm sure we could find it! Here, try it on. I promise it'll make you feel like a queen."

"I—I don't know—"

"Ah, go on," Adam cajoled. "That stubborn woman of mine won't give you a minute's peace if you don't try it on. She even had the maid who cleaned our rooms try that ring on."

"Well—if you're sure—" Tavia reached out, took the sparkling ring from Jewel's hand and slipped it onto her finger, sure this was the closest she'd ever come to wearing such a beautiful and expensive ring.

Jewel gave her a big smile. "See? Didn't I tell you?"

Tavia held out her hand, gazing at the huge stones. "Your engagement ring is the most beautiful ring I've ever seen. You're right! It does make you feel like a queen."

"You should have seen Adam propose." Jewel jabbed at her fiancé's shoulder. "He was so cute. He—"

"Hang on!" Adam's face suddenly grew serious. "There's a big eighteen-wheeler coming up fast behind us. I hope the guy's smart enough not to try to pass us on this curve."

Chapter Two

Beck hated this stretch of road. The grade at this point through the Rockies was exceptionally steep. He glanced at his watch. No trouble, he'd make his deadline in plenty of time.

Noticing an SUV in front of him, the fancy top-of-the-line kind with leather seats, big tires and a little pickup bed in the back, he smiled. Instead of numbers, the license tag read Adams-Toy. Pretty expensive toy, I'd say! He eased down on the brake.

But nothing happened.

What's wrong, Baby? The dependable truck he'd been driving for the past three years didn't respond. A feeling of panic crept through him and he hit the brakes again. Not too hard. From his years of experience, he knew if he pressed them too suddenly they might lock and that could spell disaster. Ignoring his efforts, the truck continued to move forward as if it had a mind of its own, its immense weight propelling it onward faster and faster as it descended the hill. His heart quickened with fear and trepidation as a cold sweat dampened his forehead. *God, do something! Please do something!*

The sudden blaring of the truck's air horn caused all eyes to turn in its direction.

"I think the guy's lost his brakes!" Adam gasped, his grip tightening on the steering wheel.

Terror seized Tavia's heart as she watched the oncoming truck through the rear window. "He's going to hit us! I know he is!"

"Adam! Pull off the road and let him by!" Jewel's shrill voice echoed through the inside of the truck.

"I'm trying!" Adam screamed back, "but the embankment is too steep! We'll flip over!"

Tavia wanted to watch, to make sure Adam would be able to get off the road in time, but she couldn't. Her eyes were fixed on the rapidly approaching truck, sure they were all going to die.

Beck geared down, but the truck continued to barrel forward, ever closer to the SUV.

He'd lost control.

Forty tons of steel hurtled forward of its own volition like a heat-seeking missile, and there was nothing he could do about it but watch and pray.

Beck stared through the windshield at the fancy SUV just seconds ahead of him on the road. I sounded my horn. Why doesn't the guy pull over? Try to get out of my way? He has to see me!

He sounded the horn again then glanced at the radio. What good would calling for help do? No one could help him now. He was all alone in the cab with a full load, careening totally out of control. He knew there'd be an emergency turn-off ramp down the road a couple of miles. He'd seen it hundreds of times. If it wasn't for that SUV in front of him, he might be able to make it there.

"Get out of the way! Move it!" he screamed out at the top of his lungs as he gave a long, loud blare of his horn and waved one arm frantically across the wind-shield. *"Dear Lord! Don't let those innocent people die because of me! Help me!"* he shouted out.

It's too late! The realization struck him like a sucker punch as they rounded a curve. "If I hit these people, they won't have a chance!"

He watched in horror as the distance between the two vehicles lessened, feeling helpless to do anything now but continue to hope and pray—no more in control than a mere spectator.

The brakes still weren't taking hold.

Even the Jake brake wasn't helping.

"Move it!" Beck yelled as he flailed his hand wildly across the windshield again. "Go left! Cross the road! Take the ditch! Take the ditch!"

The SUV made a slight move to the left, then a wild swing to the right, as if the driver was out of control and trying to compensate, then left again, but it was too late.

Much too late.

Beck white-knuckled the steering wheel as the truck rammed into the back of the vehicle, shoving it along as if it were a mere toy. He wanted to close his eyes, to pretend it wasn't happening, but it was and he had a front row seat. Within seconds, his bumper was crushing the SUV's rear end as easily as if it were a paper cup. The ugly sounds of the screeching Jake brake and crunching metal were deafening to his ears.

Beck clutched the steering wheel, holding on for dear life as his huge bumper pushed the mass of twisted metal down the road ahead of him, unable to do anything but ride it out and blame himself for going ahead and driving the truck after he'd suspected a problem. Although he could no longer see the passengers, he knew they must be in total panic.

The SUV continued to veer to the right, coming closer and closer to the edge of the road and the guardrail that edged itself along the deep gorge, the truck's heavy bumper twisting the vehicle's rear end around to the front like a bump-em car at a carnival. Beck maintained his death-grip hold on the steering wheel as if just by squeezing it he could regain some sense of domination.

But it didn't work.

He gulped in a breath of air and released one hand

long enough to wipe the sweat from his eyes. That guardrail would never hold!

While casting a hurried glance into the rearview mirror, Beck felt the cab begin to shift. Just as he'd suspected, the deadweight of the loaded trailer began to drift sideways, pulling him with it. *"Oh, God, no! Don't let it jackknife!"* he yelled out, knowing nothing short of a miracle from God Himself would keep this from happening. The SUV was in the truck's clutches, going wherever the eighteen-wheeler wanted to take it.

"Oh, Lord, if they go over the side, they won't have a chance! Don't let it happen! Please! Don't let it happen!"

A shower of sparks shot into the air as high as Beck's windshield as the SUV smashed sideways into the guardrail, still being scooted along at breakneck speed by the cab's massive bumper.

Beck gasped in horror as the passenger in the back seat was hurled through a window into the air, tossed along the edge of the guardrail like a rag doll being discarded by an uninterested child.

He felt bile rise in his throat and thought he was going to vomit. "No! No! This can't be happening!" If only he could do something!

Watching in what felt like slow motion, what he'd feared the most happened.

The guardrail gave way.

With nothing to stop it, the battered and beaten SUV

straddled the rocky ledge for only a few feet, then plummeted into the deep canyon below.

Though nearly out of his mind with grief and guilt, and taking time for only a quick glance over the canyon's rim, Beck continued to fight the truck as it rapidly cascaded down the descending road toward the turnout.

Then, as if it had taken on a mind of its own, the truck made a sudden swerve to the left, crossed the road and headed for the rocky embankment. That was the last thing Beck remembered.

Tavia couldn't breathe. Something was filling her mouth and nostrils. She felt herself drifting in a swirling pit of darkness. *Where am I? Why can't I breathe? My head is pounding. Black. Everything black. Am I dead? Am I in hell?*

Slowly, she tried to open her eyes, but the intense pain made it impossible, so she lay motionless instead, trying to put things together, staring at the blackness and the wisps of light that seemed to come and go in fleeting, erratic shafts.

"I think she's coming around," a female voice said. "I'm almost certain she blinked."

"I hope so. They've been so worried about her," another answered.

She felt a hand on her arm, shaking her gently. *Hurt. I hurt.*

"Can you hear me? If you can hear me, try to open your eyes."

Can't open them. They hurt. My head hurts. My chest hurts. Arm.

"She's got to be all right," a man's voice interjected. "I'm not sure that woman would make it if they lost her, too."

I hear you, I hear you. Tavia wanted to shout out the words, but they wouldn't come. Only darkness and those weird streaks of light. I hear you, she said within herself as she drifted off into the shadowy abyss of her mind and everything slowly faded away.

Beck checked the clock on the Boulder Community Hospital wall for the fifth time in the past five minutes. 8:30 p.m. He stared at his breakfast. He'd asked the nurse to leave his tray. He knew he ought to eat. His body would heal better with proper nutrition, but he wasn't hungry. His every thought was centered on the woman on the third floor. When he'd asked the nurse to check on her, she had told him she was in a coma. What a tragedy. If only he could have avoided the accident. He'd never be able to forget her face. He'd even dreamt about it. Dreamt about those big, round blue eyes staring up at him through the rear window of that oversize SUV. Would he have that same dream every night for the rest of his life?

He'd lain awake for hours after that dream, reliving

every second, wondering if he could have done anything differently to avoid that accident. But he'd been trained for situations like that. He'd done everything by the book. No one could have done more than he had. But if that were true, why was he carrying so much guilt?

He had to go to her room, to see for himself if she had awakened from the coma. After persuading one of the nurses to get him a wheelchair, Beck headed for the third floor.

He rolled his chair up beside her bed and sat staring at the small portion of the woman's face that wasn't covered by a bandage. Just seeing her arm secured by a removable cast, a tube going down her throat, and listening to the incessant beep, beep, beeping of the machines, made his heart fill with agony. *Lord, spare this woman's life. Don't take her from these people who love her. They've already lost their son. Don't take his fiancée, too! And, please, God, I need Your touch. Not for my broken leg or the cut on my head. Those will heal in time. I need You to take away this terrible feeling of guilt. I know Dr. and Mrs. Flint don't hold me responsible for the death of their son—I did all I could—but, because of me and the failure of the brakes on my truck, their son is dead and this young woman is lying here in a coma!*

"You'd better get back to your room," the nurse on duty told him a half hour later as she entered the room and adjusted the drip on the IV. "You've been here longer than you should have, considering your own condition."

He inched his chair closer to the bed, his eyes still riveted on its still occupant. "Just a few more minutes? Please?"

The nurse placed her hand on her hip, her voice showing concern. "You've been through a traumatic ordeal yourself, and you've still got quite a knot on that head. How is the leg doing?"

"I'm okay." He gestured toward the bed. "It's her I'm worried about."

She gave him a frown. "We're all worried about her."

The woman lying in the bed suddenly let out a stifled cough, then seemed to gag. Beck lunged forward, not sure what he could do to help. Was she coming out of the coma?

The nurse put a comforting hand on his shoulder. "It's all right. Folks do that sometimes when they're in a coma. It's nothing to worry about."

He leaned back in the chair and rubbed at his forehead, for a moment nearly forgetting about the swelling and the stitches. "It's a miracle she's alive. If you'd seen that—"

She waggled a finger at him. "You have to try to put that out of your mind, Mr. Brewster. It's not good for you to dwell on it. You need to concentrate on getting well."

"Please, let me stay a little longer." He shifted in the chair, his leg muscles reminding him of the excessive amount of stress and strain he'd put on them, pressing the pedal and trying to get the brakes to take hold.

She tilted her head with a scowl. "I shouldn't let you stay."

"I know, but she might wake up, so I want to be here."

After a glance at her watch, she shrugged. "Oh, all right. Fifteen minutes more, but that's it. Her family is down in the cafeteria. They'll be back any time now. The doctor said only two visitors in the room at a time. No more."

"I'll leave when they get here." Beck gave her a nod and a smile of thanks before turning his interest back to the still form of the injured woman. Gazing at what little of her face was showing, he wondered what she really looked like. It was hard to tell with all the bandages and that tube. He could barely see the color of her hair. Was she young? Old? Short? Tall? He'd caught only a brief glimpse of her as she'd stared up at him out that back window. All he could remember about her was the terror he'd seen in her eyes.

"Wake up. Please, wake up," he pleaded as he reached out and carefully touched her arm. "If I could, I'd gladly trade places with you."

Except for the constant beeping of the machines, the room remained silent.

He gently stroked her swollen hand. "I'm—I'm so sorry. If it weren't for me—"

"You can't blame yourself, Beck."

Startled, he pulled his hand away and turned toward the voice. "Hello, Dr. Flint. H—how's your wife doing?"

The man raised a hand to his brow, his forehead creasing with concern. "Not so good. She's not in good health anyway, and this whole thing hit her pretty hard. Both of us. She'll be here in a minute. She stopped at the ladies' room to freshen up."

The quiver in the man's voice went straight to Beck's heart.

Dr. Flint moved to the opposite side of the bed and, through misty eyes, stared quietly at the bandaged face.

"If it weren't for me, your son—"

James Flint put a cautioning finger to his lips, then said in a low whisper, "Shh. We have to be careful what we say around her. The doctor said sometimes, even though people are in a coma, they claim later they could hear what was being said in the room. We don't want her to know about him until the doctor says she's ready and can handle it. I've already warned Annie to be careful about what she says."

Beck nodded.

The two men moved to the foot of the bed and continued their conversation in hushed tones. "You can't go on blaming yourself, Beck. It wasn't your fault. Both my wife and I realize that. From what the sheriff told us of his ongoing investigation, you did the best you could to get that truck stopped. In fact, the sheriff said it looked as if the accident could have been a whole lot worse if you hadn't maneuvered that truck to the side of the road like you did. I'm just glad you remembered Adam's license plate so they could trace it and let us know what happened. I'd bought that SUV for him as an early graduation present, so it was still registered in my name. I'd even had those silly words, *Adam's toy,* put on that plate."

Beck stared at the motionless figure in the bed. He had done all he could, but it hadn't been enough. A young man in the prime of his life had died, and a woman lay badly injured and in a coma. He almost felt embarrassed to be alive. Why God had spared his sorry life and taken theirs he'd never understand. At least, not until he met his Savior face-to-face and could ask Him. He tried to speak, but his throat tightened and held his words captive.

Dr. Flint placed his hand on Beck's shoulder, pausing as if to get control of his emotions before going on. "From what the sheriff said about the looks of that truck of yours, I'd say you were lucky to get out of it alive." He gestured toward the woman in the bed. "Good thing she wasn't wearing her seatbelt. If she'd had it on, she might not have been thrown out the window and ended up in that—"

"I'm concerned about your wife, Dr. Flint." Beck blinked hard, his own emotions about to get the better of him, too.

"Annie hasn't slept a wink since—well, you know. Her cardiologist checked her over this morning before we came to the hospital. Her heart is as weak as ever, and he's worried about the strain all of this has put on her. We have to keep a close watch on her and protect her as much as possible." He motioned toward Tavia. "I think all that's kept Annie going is the sweet little girl lying in that bed. The two of us can't understand why God would take our Adam, but we're so thankful He didn't take Adam's fiancée, too."

Beck gazed at the woman, trying to imagine what her face would look like without the contortions of fear he'd seen on it. "I'll bet she's as pretty as her name."

"I—I don't know." The man frowned as he gazed at the bandaged face. "Our son thought she was the most beautiful woman in the world, but my wife and I have never met her."

Beck stared up at him, confused by his words. "You've never met her?"

"No, she and Adam had recently become engaged, but we hadn't had a chance to meet her yet. That's why he was bringing her home. I couldn't even tell the hospital if she had insurance, but once I told them I'd be responsible for her bills if she didn't, and signed a few papers, they were appeased."

Beck let out a deep sigh. "Seems sad that a hospital would be concerned about getting their money when someone is injured."

"I know, but as a doctor, I understand. Hospital care is expensive. Someone has to pay the bill."

"You have seen pictures of your son's fiancée, haven't you?"

Dr. Flint shook his head. "Actually, no, I haven't. I just hope her face—" The man stopped midsentence, his eyes once again gazing at the still figure. "I'm sure she'll be fine. The CAT scan showed no brain damage. That's a good sign. The doctor said they're evaluating her neuro status every couple of hours. She's responding to stimulation. Her pupils are equal and reactive to light. We have to keep trusting God to answer our prayers."

"It scared me when she sort of gagged and coughed, but the nurse said that's okay."

"Yes, that's normal. I guess if I had a tube going down my throat, I'd gag, too."

A trim, haggard-looking woman in her late fifties moved slowly into the room, her face showing evidence of the many tears she'd shed. Though she offered him a weak smile, Beck could tell it was with great effort. He knew, first-hand, there hadn't been anything in her life the past twenty-four hours that would cause a genuine smile. "Hello, Mrs. Flint."

James Flint leaned close to his wife and whispered, "Remember, we have to watch what we say around her. She may be able to hear us."

She nodded. "How are you doing, Beck?"

"I'm okay, Mrs. Flint."

Annie Flint's husband's arms circled her and pulled her close. "I was just telling Beck that Adam and Jewel were engaged."

Annie leaned into her husband, her eyes overflowing with fresh tears. "They were so happy."

The tremor in her voice tore at Beck, pulling at his heart and bringing back his penitent feelings of responsibility.

James shrugged and pulled her even closer, his whisper cracking with emotion, "I'm just thankful Jewel was spared."

Annie pulled away from her husband and moved to the bed, touching her almost-daughter-in-law's arm. "She has to be special. Our Adam loved her enough to want to spend the rest of his life with her." She whirled around quickly and pressed her face into her husband's chest as deep, uncontrolled sobs racked at her body. "Oh, J-James! This is so hard! Why would God take our son?"

A shrill beeping sent the room's occupants into sudden panic.

Chapter Three

*V*oices.

I hear voices and some sort of sound. A beeping sound.

Tavia tried to concentrate, but her fuzzy brain wouldn't allow it. No matter how hard she tried to zero in on the distant noises, they drifted in and out like a radio station whose signal was being lost. She struggled to open her eyes but nothing happened. It was as if she was in a deep, deep pit, with no control and no way out. She even tried to scream, to call out to someone—anyone, but her vocal cords remained still, her commands not getting through to them. Help me! Someone help me!

Do they even know I'm here? If I can't see them, does that mean they can't see me? Oh, where am I?

Carefully pushing every other thought from her mind, she tried to listen to the voices, but the sounds were getting weaker and weaker. No matter how hard she willed herself to hang on, she felt herself slipping deeper and deeper into the pit. No! I want to stay here. I have to hang on. But to what? There's nothing to grip. No handles. No rung on the ladder.

"There's no need for concern," she heard a woman's voice say through the haze circulating in her mind. "It's time to change her IV, that's all."

Tavia willed herself to tighten her grip on the walls, clinging to them frantically. She listened, but again the words were drifting in and out. She felt herself falling—going backward, spinning out of control. What would happen if she hit bottom? Everything was dark—so dark. She hated the darkness. Nearly everything bad that had ever happened to her had happened in the darkness.

"Go back to your room, Beck. You need to get some rest."

Beck? Who is Beck? Tavia struggled to find something solid to hang on to—something to stop her fall. Though they were faint now, she could still hear the voices, but it was impossible to make out the words. Beck, Beck, Beck. She repeated the word over and over in her head until the pit claimed her once more.

"Annie and I are going to stay for a while."

Beck gave James a dubious look. "Are you sure she's up to it?"

"She's out of her mind with grief—we both are—but she insisted on coming here today."

Beck grabbed on to the wheels on the side of his chair and spun himself around. "I promised the nurse I'd leave as soon as you two got here. You will let me know if there's any change, won't you?"

"Yes, of course. You know we will." James motioned downward. "By the way, that leg bothering you much? I see you wince now and then."

"It's doing okay. My injuries are nothing compared to hers. With those pins holding it together, the doc said it should be fine."

"How about the bump on your head?"

Beck's fingers touched the stitches holding together the split in his forehead. "Still sore, but it's the least of my worries. I just want this leg to get well so I can drive again. Driving is all I know."

He lingered long enough to take one last look at the still figure in the bed. Why did he have the strange feeling she was reaching out to him? He'd never even met the woman, yet he'd never forget those frightened eyes as they'd peered up at him through that window. He'd seen many a frightened deer mesmerized by his truck's powerful headlights, but none had worn the look of sheer panic she'd had as she'd stared up at him. Those eyes had pleaded for help. He hadn't been able to do a thing for her, and it had nearly killed him. In fact, he almost wished he'd died in the accident. Anything would be better than knowing his truck had killed a man, and injured this woman nearly to the point of death. Even if she made it, what would her life—

"Mr. Brewster? I'll help you if you're ready to go."

He turned quickly to find one of the nurse's aides holding on to the handle grips on his wheelchair. "Sure. Yes, thanks. I'm ready."

"You can't let this consume you, Beck." James Flint released his hold on his wife and moved to Beck's side. "Perhaps it'd be best if you stayed away for a few days, worked on getting yourself well. I'm afraid the time you spend here is depressing you, and that can't be good for you."

Beck stole another quick glance toward the tiny patch of skin showing beneath the heavy bandage. "Sir, I hope you'll allow me to keep coming. I—I can't go on with my life until I know she's—"

James cleared his throat nervously, then motioned the nurse's aide to roll Beck to the door, whispering so only Beck could hear, "I didn't want to say too much in front of Annie, but there's no telling how long Jewel may stay in that coma, and we—we may lose her yet, unless God intervenes. There's always the chance of complications."

Beck swallowed at his emotions. "I pray for her constantly. God can't let her die."

Joining them near the door, Annie wiped at her tears and circled her arms around her husband's waist, her face drawn and red from crying. "None of this makes any sense. I want my Adam back! He was too young to die. I don't understand why God, a God of love, would take him! Or why he would allow Jewel to be so severely injured."

James stroked his wife's back, his own eyes filling with tears. "I don't, either, sweetheart. I'm as angry about this as you. I'm sure God understands our anger."

Beck grimaced. "I can't begin to imagine how hard this is on the two of you. Even knowing God and being able to turn to Him, I'm having a hard time, too."

"Hopefully, we'll understand it by and by. We have to keep trusting Him, Beck, and keep praying for our little girl." James nodded to the nurse's aide. "Make sure this man takes care of himself."

The woman smiled and began to maneuver the wheelchair across the room.

Beck glanced back over his shoulder as she moved him into the hall. "Remember—if there's any change…"

James smiled. "If there's any change, we'll come after you."

Beck rode silently through the long, sterile halls, his mind fixated on Jewel Flint. Surely, since the CAT scan didn't show any serious damage or swelling, she'd come out of that coma soon. What a shock it was going to be to wake up and find Adam had died.

He waved off the nurse's aide and struggled to pull himself onto his bed when they reached his room. He wasn't used to having anyone do things for him. He'd always been that way. His dad had been a military man and had treated his family like soldiers in his platoon. Stand up straight. Speak only when you're spoken to.

Make sure you can bounce a dime off that bed when you make it. Keep those shoes shined. Say "sir" when you speak to me. He could recite hundreds of commands his father had enforced. But, looking back, none of those things had hurt him or his siblings. They'd all turned out to be a pretty good, independent bunch of kids. All five of them.

"Ready for a pain pill?" the nurse who'd just come into his room asked. "I see on your chart your doctor has prescribed them for you but you haven't been taking them."

He shook his head. "Don't need them. Thanks."

His body felt as if it needed them. Everything ached, but he wasn't about to take any pills that weren't absolutely necessary. He'd heard too many horror stories about guys getting hooked on them, and he wasn't going to be one of them. His livelihood was driving a truck. Besides, pain pills couldn't stop those big round eyes from haunting him.

"Well, it's up to you. Let us know if you change your mind." The nurse placed the chart on the nightstand and moved to take his vitals.

He watched in silence. "Think I'll make it?" he asked with a shy grin when she finally finished and picked up a pen to write the information on his chart.

"What do you think?"

"I think I'll feel a whole lot better when I get out of here and can walk normally again."

* * *

Tavia struggled though the mist, reaching upward with all her might. She had to get out of that dark pit before it consumed her. What was that noise? A swishing of some kind. Suddenly she felt warm. She'd been so cold, now she felt warm. Why?

"Well, little lady, is this going to be the day you come back to us? I've opened the blinds. Can you feel the sunlight on your face? It's a beautiful day outside. Clear. Crisp. How about a nice warm washcloth on your face? How would that feel?"

Tavia could hear the sound of running water and someone humming, then footsteps shuffling across a floor. "As soon as we get you all cleaned up, I'll rub some nice lotion on you. Would you like that? Oh, by the way, that man in the wheelchair was here again this morning. He wanted to know how you were doing."

Man? What man?

"He sure is interested in you. I had to chase him out of here so I could give you your bath." There was a pause. "He doesn't look so good himself. Broken leg, big knot on his head and who knows what else, but I guess he'll be going home soon. Umm, let me see. I think his name was Dick? Bart? Beck? Something like that."

Beck? That's the man I heard talking!

"Come on, Missy. Let's turn you on your side. We need to pull this gown off and get you into a clean one. There you go. Now, let me lift your arm."

Pain! I can't stand the pain. With one final thrust, she sent herself hurtling upward, willing her eyes to open.

There was the sound of something suddenly hitting the floor, a metal dish or pan, a gasp, footsteps moving away from her, then silence.

Wait! Don't leave me! Tavia felt her pain increase and her strength waning, but she couldn't give up now. Not when she was so close. Come back!

"I'm sure I saw her eyelids flutter!"

"Let me take a look," a second woman said. "Perhaps it was just an involuntary muscular reaction. That happens sometimes."

"No, I don't think so. I'm sure she was trying to open her eyes."

I am trying! Watch, I'll do it again! With every ounce of strength she could summon, Tavia struggled to force her eyelids open. It was so hard, but she had to do it. She had to let them know before she slipped back into the tunnel.

"There! See! She did it again."

"You're right! Get the doctor. Hurry!"

Tavia drew back as the light flooded in, bathing her like a refreshing wave of ocean water. She'd made it! She'd reached the top! Now, if she could just hold on. But she was tired, so tired. She needed to sleep. To sleep.

"Can you hear me?"

Startled, Tavia pulled herself up to the rim again, holding on tightly as she strained toward the man's voice. I hear you. Throat hurts. Why can't I swallow?

"Come on, young lady. Open your eyes. I'm Dr. Stevens. I'm here to help you."

Dr. Stevens? Am I in a hospital? Why? Pictures, like a slide show on a screen, flashed through her mind, each lasting only a split second. A truck. The sound of a loud horn.

"Come on, try to open your eyes. Come back to us."

"Shall I get her family?" the woman's voice asked.

"Not yet. Let's be sure first. We don't want to disappoint them."

I don't have a family.

"We need you to open your eyes wide. Can you do that for me?"

I'm trying! I'm trying!

"Atta girl! Come on."

It's—it's so hard.

Someone touched her arm. Now she had something to hold on to. Something to keep her from slipping back into that abyss. Move! Blink! Let them know you hear them!

"She moved her good arm, Doctor!"

The excitement in the woman's voice made Tavia want to shout. Finally, someone was helping her out of the pit.

"Can you move your arm again?"

An excruciating pain shot through her as Tavia pressed her eyelids together and lifted with all her might. She wanted to cry out.

"Oh, Doctor, she did it, and I saw her eyelids move again."

The woman sounded almost as excited as Tavia felt. I've got to open my eyes. I've got to!

"Close the blinds," the man's voice ordered. "It's too bright in here. The sun is shining right in her face."

Tavia heard the swish of the blinds closing.

"Open those eyes," a kindly voice said through the fog still swirling around her.

Slowly, Tavia opened them, peering through her lashes at first, then wider. Why wouldn't her right eye open as easily as her left? A man stood close to her, giving her a pleasant smile.

"Ah, much better." The man's smile broadened. "Your family will be glad to see you're back with us again. You're in Boulder Community Hospital. We airlifted you here."

Tavia flinched at the word *family*. I don't have a family. There must be some mistake.

"I finally talked them into going to the cafeteria to have breakfast, but they should be back soon," the doctor said, still smiling at her. "I need to check those beautiful eyes. Let's see how they react to light."

He pulled a small flashlight from his pocket and pointed it at her face. Tavia blinked as he moved it from one side to the other. She'd been in the darkness for such a long time and the light was so bright.

Finally, he turned the light off and slipped it back in his pocket. "Looking good!"

"Oh, you're awake!" said a female voice.

Tavia squinted up into the smiling face of an attractive, if frail-looking, woman, who seemed to appear out of nowhere, so unexpected was her entry.

"We were so worried." There was a man standing by the woman's side and he patted Tavia's shoulder. "You don't know how happy this makes us."

"You've come back to us." The woman, her eyes filled with tears, lifted her hair to one side and bent to place a kiss on Tavia's cheek. "I can hardly wait to tell Grandpa. He's been praying for you, too."

Why would these people pray for me? Are they some do-gooders from a local church? Do they have the wrong room? And who is Grandpa?

The man's face took on a serious cast. "How is she, Dr. Stevens?"

"I'd say considering her injuries, she's doing quite well. Her vitals are decent, but with the kind of trauma she's been through, we'll continue to intubate her and ventilate her until she's completely stable. Maybe only a day or so. Now that she's come around she'll be in quite a bit of pain with those broken ribs and her fractured arm, but we can deal with that. She's bound to be a bit disoriented at times," he went on, "but that should go away in a few days. If she keeps responding as she is now, I should be able to take that tube out by tomorrow or the next day."

The man released a heavy sigh. "You have no idea how glad we are to hear this."

"Well, I'll leave you to visit with her. I have other patients to see."

The couple gave the doctor wide smiles, though the woman kept dabbing at her eyes with a hanky. She looked as if she'd been crying for days. "I'm so happy to see your lovely eyes. I don't know what I would have done if—"

"Now, Annie—" The man wrapped his arms about the woman and held her close. "Don't even think that way. God answered our prayers and brought her back to us."

Tavia's gaze flitted from one to the other and back again. What about Adam? What about Jewel? Did that nice couple send you here to cheer me up? Yes, that must be it. Adam and Jewel asked you to come.

The woman began to weep hysterically. "Oh, James, what if she hadn't—"

"But she did make it, Annie." Tears rolled down the man's cheeks as he spoke. "We have to take comfort in her survival."

Though she didn't know them, their tears made Tavia want to cry, too, at the deep, horrible pain evident in their voices. But why?

The man gave Tavia a look of concern. "I think you've had enough excitement for one day." He cupped his hand gently about her shoulder. "We'll go now and let you get some rest, but we'll be back in a few hours."

Annie rubbed her tears away with her fingertips before bending to kiss Tavia's cheek again. "I hate to leave you."

James grabbed on to his wife's hand, tugging her away. "She needs her rest, Annie, and so do you."

"I know, but—"

He motioned her toward the door. "We'll come back later, I promise."

Annie blew her a kiss as the pair backed out of the hospital room, leaving Tavia with puzzled thoughts and unanswered questions. Did these people have her mixed up with someone else? Surely, they could tell she wasn't someone they knew. It was all so confusing.

The darkness. The tunnel. The hospital room. A couple who said they loved her and prayed for her. None of it made any sense. The room began to spin again, making her dizzy. The constant *beep, beep, beep* of the machines was grating on her nerves.

"Hi."

Slightly turning her head, she peered into the face of yet another stranger. A man in a wheelchair, with a bandage on his head and a small vase of white daisies balanced between his knees.

"They said you were awake. I've been so worried about you." He placed the vase on the nightstand. "I brought these for you. They're not much, but they were all the hospital gift shop had to offer."

You've been worried about me, too? And you brought me flowers? Why? Are you a friend of those people who were just here? Annie and James?

"I was here earlier, but I guess you didn't hear me. I—I want you to know how sorry I am. If it weren't for me, you wouldn't have been injured. Honest, I did everything I could to avoid the accident, but there wasn't anything I could do. The truck just kept barreling down the road."

Accident! This must be the man I heard earlier. Tavia concentrated with all her might, trying to bring up any details of an accident that might be buried deep within her mind. Why was she having so much trouble keeping things straight? And, she hurt. Oh, how she hurt. Just the slightest movement was sheer agony. Pain. Why doesn't someone give me something for the pain?

"You were looking up at me through the rear window of that SUV." The man in the wheelchair paused as a tear tumbled down his cheeks. "I—I figured you wouldn't make it. But, praise God, you did!"

If only she could get the words out, ask him about the couple who had given her a ride, but she couldn't. Something deep in her throat prevented it.

The man worked his wheelchair up close to her bed, then carefully placed a hand on her arm. "I shouldn't have mentioned the accident. I didn't mean to upset you. I'd better leave now, but I'll be back. You do what the doctor says so you can get well. I'll be praying for you." With that, he maneuvered the chair from the room.

Tavia watched him go. All my life no one has cared if I lived or died, now three strangers are concerned about me. Unable to keep her eyes open any longer, she felt herself sinking, ever so slowly, backward. But this time was different. The pit wasn't pulling her down, she just felt tired. Sleepy. Sl-ee-py.

Chapter 4

Tavia was awakened by the cheery sound of a woman's voice.

"Someone must think you're pretty special!"

With tremendous effort, Tavia turned her head and stared at the woman crossing the room toward her, her hands filled with colorful flowers.

"What a lovely bouquet! Everyone said it made the entire hallway smell like roses." The woman gave her a warm smile as she placed the lovely wicker basket full of colorful, sweet-smelling flowers on the night table.

Wait! Don't leave them here. Those can't be for me! No one has ever sent me a big bouquet.

The woman drew in a deep whiff of the sweet fragrance. "Would you like me to read the card to you?"

Narrowing her eyes, Tavia tried to focus on the woman. The volunteer fanned a hand toward her and gave her a lopsided grin. "Silly me. I should've realized you couldn't answer me with that tube going down your throat. Of course, you want me to read the card to you. How else would you know who sent these beautiful flowers?"

She pulled the card from the little envelope with a flourish. "It says, 'We're so thankful you're alive. Your room is ready. As soon as the doctor says it's okay, we'll be taking you home.' And it's signed, Love, Mom and Dad. Now isn't that just the sweetest thing? Your mother and father must be wonderful people."

Those flowers can't be for me! My parents died years ago! Tavia tried to blink back tears, but it was impossible. If only someone did care enough about her to send flowers, but that was nothing but wishful thinking.

The nice lady hurried to her side and pulled a tissue from the box on her tray. "I know you're hurting, honey, but things will get better. Honest, they will."

But, I don't even know these people!

"I'll be going now. I have several more bouquets to deliver, but none as pretty as the one I brought to you. You take care now, and get well soon so you can go home."

Tavia gave the volunteer one last frantic look. Getting one bouquet had startled her. Receiving two was utterly impossible! That nice lady who delivered the flowers had to have made a mistake. Tavia stared at the basket of flowers. It was the most beautiful bouquet she'd ever seen. The kind people would send for grand openings, or to celebrities on awards night. Why would anyone spend that kind of money on her?

The last thing she remembered before drifting off was the sweet scent of roses.

It took a few minutes for Tavia to focus her eyes as she stared at the blinds on the window. Her puffed-up right eye still refused to cooperate. How long had she been asleep? It was still light outside, but the sun was low in the sky, turning everything into a rosy haze. She turned her head slowly, painfully, toward the other side of the bed. A man in a wheelchair sat staring at her. Finally he spoke.

"I don't want to bother you. I'll go if you want me to. You've been asleep for several hours."

"Well, our little sweetheart is awake!"

Tavia glanced toward the door at the sound of familiar voices. There had been a constant string of people in and out of her room—people she didn't know. This time, Dr. Stevens, Annie and James filed in, with an older stranger following close behind. Annie's eyes were still swollen from crying and her nose was red. "Oh, good, you got our flowers."

Annie placed a box on the chair, then bent to plant a kiss on Tavia's cheek. You're the ones who sent that big basket of flowers? But why? You don't even know me.

The older man stuck out his hand toward the man in the wheelchair. "I'm James's father. You must be Beck. James and Annie told me all about you."

Beck hung his head as he shook the man's hand. "Yes, I was driving the truck, sir."

James's father nodded. "I know, but from what they've told me, you did all you could to avoid the accident. It just wasn't enough."

How are Adam and Jewel? Please, someone tell me! Are they in this hospital, too? Have you just come from seeing them?

"I'll never forgive myself, sir." Beck stiffened. "That accident will haunt me the rest of my days."

Tavia watched as he blinked back tears. She couldn't remember when she'd last seen a man his age cry, much less a big man like Beck.

The older man eyed the wheelchair. "How long you gonna have to be in that thing?"

"Doc says I can start walking on this cast tomorrow, so he'll be releasing me."

Annie tugged on her father-in-law's sleeve. "Come and meet our miracle girl." Together they moved up close to Tavia.

"We're so thankful God spared your life by letting you be thrown out that window before—" James gulped hard, nearly choking on his words as he gazed at her.

I was thrown out a window? I don't remember. It's all so hazy.

Grandpa sidled up to the bed, wrapping his arm about his daughter-in-law's shoulders. "Didn't God say all things worked together for good?"

"But this, Dad?" Annie pulled a fresh tissue from the box and wiped at her tears. "What good could come of all of this? I know I shouldn't question God, but I do. I don't understand this at all!"

You're Adam's parents! Adam asked you to come and check on me! That was so thoughtful of him.

"She's going to recover. Considering how close she came to not making it, that's good," Grandpa offered.

His words brought the truth home for Tavia. The pain in my chest is killing me, and I ache all over, but I'm alive! But what of Jewel and Adam? I need to know.

"I'm afraid we're upsetting her with all this talk about the accident." James tugged on his wife's arm and pointed to the box on the chair. "Annie, why don't you show her what you brought?"

Annie dabbed at her bloodshot eyes with a fresh tissue, donning a grin that even Tavia, who barely knew the woman, could tell was only put on for her benefit. Annie looked waxen and wan—as if she would collapse at any moment. "I've brought you a few things."

Tavia watched as she took the lid off the box and began pulling things out and placing them on the foot of her bed.

"A few soft, silky nightgowns, so you won't have to wear those awful hospital gowns. A robe and matching slippers. I guessed at your size. I hope they fit. Here's a makeup bag with a new toothbrush, toothpaste, cleansing cream, moisturizer and some other things you'll need." Annie rezipped the bag then moved closer, carefully lifting a lock of Tavia's hair from her forehead and giving her a tender smile. "When you're up to it, I'll help you wash and fix your hair."

Tavia wanted to thank her, but all she could do was nod a bit.

"If there's anything you need, just let me know and I'll get it for you." Annie turned away quickly, pulling out the drawer on the nightstand and placing the things she'd brought inside, but Tavia could tell she'd begun to sob again.

James lightly clamped a quivering hand on Tavia's shoulder. "We—we—" He swallowed hard. "There—there is something you should know. Even though Dr. Stevens said it would be all right to tell you, I—I'm not sure you're up to it—but you have to hear it, and—we—we thought it best if you heard it from us."

What? What do I need to hear? What else could possibly have happened?

The three men staring at her looked on the verge of tears. Dr. Stevens, with a look of concern, had moved from the foot of the bed to stand beside Annie who was already sobbing her heart out. Tavia glanced from one to the other, then back to James. Their serious faces scared her, and she still couldn't figure out why they were all there. Especially, Dr. Stevens. *Come on—tell me! I need to know. Is this about Adam and Jewel?*

James swallowed at a lump in his throat, then with a quick intake of breath, blurted out, "Adam didn't make it."

The words struck terror to Tavia's heart. Adam died? The room began to whirl again and she felt faint.

"He's gone. Our Adam is gone."

Oh, no! Not Adam! Not that nice young man. Tavia's head reeled as her stomach began to lurch and her eyes filled with tears. I lived? And he died? She felt herself shuddering and couldn't stop. What about Jewel? Tell me about her! How bad was she hurt? Her eyes skipped to the Flints. He was their only child. These poor people must be devastated!

"After you were thrown out of the SUV, it—" Adam's father paused and stared off into space, unable go on.

You've already told me that! Tell me about Jewel! She stared at James. After grabbing hold of the back of Annie's chair and pressing his eyelids shut, James went on, his voice a mere whisper. "His truck—"

Grandpa grabbed ahold of his son's arm. "It fell into the deep canyon— Adam never had a chance."

Burying his face in his hands, Beck began to sob audibly. "I'm so sorry! If only I'd been able to stop my truck—"

Grandpa moved quickly to Beck and placed a steadying hand on his shoulder. Then in a voice that betrayed his own emotions, said, "You did all you could. For— for some reason we don't understand, God wanted to take Adam home."

Stirred by his father's words, James knelt in front of his wife, cradling her face against him as she wept, his own tears flowing unashamedly. Swallowing hard, he sent a slight smile toward Tavia. "My dear child, you are a true blessing from God. Having you here with us is—is like having a little bit of our son. Though we've lost our beloved son, Jewel, you have become the daughter we've always wanted."

Chapter Five

❧

Their words hit Tavia in the gut like a prize-fighter's fist. *Why would you call me Jewel? I'm not Jewel.* She tried to give her head a vicious shake, but with the ventilator tube in her throat it was impossible. Her heartbeat pounded in her ears and her eyes burned with tears. *I'm not Jewel! I'm Tavia! Why do you think I'm Jewel?*

"You'll never know how much it means to both Annie and me to know that, even though it was touch and go there for a while, you've made it."

Tavia stared at James. *You've got to find Jewel! No wonder no one has mentioned her whereabouts since the accident. They think I'm her. Where is she? Surely not lying out there in that canyon.*

Dr. Stevens momentarily left Annie and moved to Tavia's side, gripping her forearm between his palms. "We knew this would upset you, but you had to know.

It wouldn't be fair to let you think Adam was alive. I'm going to ask the nurse to give you something to calm you down."

No! I don't want to calm down. I want all of you to know the truth! I'm not Jewel Mallory! I'm Tavia! Tavia MacRae! You have to make these good people understand I'm not who they think I am. This can't be happening.

James took both Annie's hands and tugged her to her feet. "Maybe this would be a good time to give Jewel the other thing you've brought her."

With a trembling hand and her eyes overflowing with tears, Annie reached into her purse, unzipped a small compartment, and pulled out a tiny plastic bag.

"The people here at the hospital gave this to us the night the ambulance brought you here." James explained when Annie's voice cracked and failed her. "Annie thought it would make you feel better to know it was safe."

Her insides still quivering from the horrible news, Tavia frowned through her tears as she watched Annie plunge her slender fingers into the bag. What could possibly make me feel better, now that I know that Adam is dead?

Annie stood weeping for a moment, as if trying to regain some sense of composure before drawing something out. From her weakened appearance, Tavia was afraid the frail woman would collapse at any moment and now understood why Dr. Stevens was in the room.

"Your engagement ring—" Annie paused and swallowed hard, once more filled with an overwhelming grief.

"I asked the hospital staff to take it off your hand—" Annie's voice faded into nothingness as James pulled his wife close.

That's it. That's why you thought I was Jewel. I was wearing her ring." Horror seized Tavia as she considered the ramifications of that goofing around. No one knew Adam had picked up a hitchhiker.

Suddenly, Annie's flattened palm went to her chest again and she stiffened, uttering an audible gasp.

Dr. Stevens rushed to her side. Turning to the nurse, he ordered, "Get her some nitroglycerin, quick!"

Her expression one of fear, Annie stood motionless, leaning against James, her eyes locked in a blank stare.

James grew wild with worry. "Hold on, sweetheart!"

Keeping her palm pressed over her heart, Annie allowed James and the doctor to help her into a chair, finally answering in a strained whisper, "Just—give me a mi-minute."

Grandpa Flint moved up beside them, his face, too, filled with great concern. He pulled the ring from his daughter-in-law's hand and dropped it in his jacket pocket. "Take it easy, Annie girl."

The nurse rushed in and helped slip the nitroglycerin tablet under Annie's tongue.

The room was silent as each person's eyes were riveted on Annie. After only a few seconds, she began to breath a little easier and a bit of color returned to her cheeks.

"Has the pain eased?" Dr. Stevens asked, hovering over her. "Are you feeling better now?"

She nodded and reached for James's hand.

"Good. I can only imagine how hard this is on you, Annie," the doctor said in a kindly way. "But you must try to calm down."

Annie's lower lip began to tremble. "I—I can't calm down. I miss Adam."

Cupping his wife's hands in his, James appeared to be fighting back his own tears. "I know, honey, but we have to be brave. That's what Adam would have wanted. All of this stress isn't good for you. You know I could never live if I didn't have you, and we have Jewel and her health to think of now. We have to be strong for her."

"He's right, Annie, and call if you need me. I mean it. Any time of the day or night, and it wouldn't hurt you to stay in bed a few days, either." Dr. Stevens shook hands with James, Beck and Grandpa, smiled at Tavia and left with the nurse at his heels.

Grandpa leaned over the foot of the bed, his forehead creased with concern. "I wish there was someone we could call for you, Jewel. You should have family with you at a time like this."

Despite the terrible excruciating pain in her side, Tavia gave her head a shake. No! There's no one. And I am not Jewel! For all your sakes, I wish I was, but I'm not! You have to understand!

James reached up and latched on to his father's elbow. "Dad, remember? Adam told us Jewel's parents died in an auto accident when she was a senior in high school. Both her parents were only children. All she has now is a few distant relatives scattered across the country that she hasn't seen since she was a baby."

Grandpa released a sigh. "Well, it seems a shame there are no kinfolk to call to let them know what's happened to her."

"That's odd to hear. Everybody has someone in their life. Even me," Beck said.

Tears flooded Tavia's eyes as she lay quietly listening, her heart aching for Adam's parents and his grandfather. In some ways, she was in the same boat as Jewel. No parents, no aunts or uncles, no one to care if she lived or died. *Someone needs to go find Jewel! She may be seriously injured and need help.*

Grandpa affectionately patted Tavia's shoulder. "You have a family now. Don't you worry. We're going to take good care of you and get you back on your feet." He leaned toward his son and said in a whisper, "Why don't you take Annie on home? She needs to rest. I'll stay here for a while then call one of my friends to come and take me home. Don't worry about this young lady. I'll take good care of her."

Tavia strained to hear their words.

"Thanks, Dad, but I'm—I'm not sure we should leave Jewel—not after telling her about Adam."

Grandpa patted his son's shoulder affectionately. "Annie needs to get home, James. Trust me. I'll watch over Jewel."

James hesitated. "What if—"

"Jewel will be fine. Go on now."

James glanced at Tavia then, turning back to his father, said, "Thanks, Dad. I don't know what we'd do without you."

Grandpa gave him a wink. "Nor do I know what I'd do without you."

James took hold of his wife's arm. "Come on, sweetheart. Let's get you home. You've had more than enough for one day."

Annie blotted her eyes with her hanky, then, her body still trembling uncontrollably, bent and kissed Tavia's cheek, telling her in a tearful whisper, "I'm so sorry, Jewel. I wish we hadn't had to tell you, but—but you had to know. You loved our Adam, too."

Look into my eyes. Can't you see I'm trying to tell you something? I'm not Jewel.

After saying goodbye, James wrapped his arm about Annie and led her out the door.

"I'd better be going, too," Beck said. "I don't know what to say, Jewel, except I'm sorry. I'll spend the rest of my life trying to make this up to you."

Oh, please, Beck. Can't you see this isn't right? I'm not Jewel. You have to make them understand!

Grandpa gave the man a reassuring pat. "You need

to take care of that leg. Don't worry about Jewel. I'll be right here."

"Yes, sir, I know you will, but please have the nurse call me—for anything."

"It's a promise." Grandpa watched Beck propel his chair through the door then circled the bed slowly, his narrowed eyes focused on Tavia. "Too bad you can't talk with that thing in your throat. There's so much I'd like to ask you about the accident. Maybe it'll help to talk about it when you're better."

Tavia felt her heartbeat quicken. *Oh, why did this have to happen? If anyone died in that wreck, it should have been me. Why would God allow me to live, and take Adam? Someone needs to find Jewel before it's too late.*

"You have to calm down, too. I know that's easier said than done, but you've been through so much yourself. All of this agitation isn't good for you." Grandpa tilted his head and peered at her. "You're a pretty little thing, I don't know why you never liked having your picture taken. But I hate to have my picture taken, too. I always look like a walrus in those things." He let loose a good-natured laugh. "Never like the handsome man I really am!"

Tavia knew his uplifting attitude was a put-on. He was doing his best to cheer her up. It made her wish she could smile back at him. *You're very kind, but I'm not pretty like Jewel is! Someone needs to find her.*

"Are you a member of the Flint family?"

Both Tavia and Grandpa's attention was drawn to the tall, gray-haired man in a Colorado State Trooper's uniform as he came into the room and removed his hat.

"Yes, sir. I'm George Flint, Adam's grandfather."

"I worked your grandson's accident, Mr. Flint. I just wanted to express my sorrow at your loss." The man nodded his head toward Tavia. "How is she doing?"

"Thanks to the Lord, she's alive. The doctor says, considering what she's gone through, she's doing remarkably well."

The trooper lowered his voice and leaned toward Grandpa. "Good thing she was thrown out of that vehicle before it went on down into that canyon. There's no way anyone who was in that SUV could have survived, not with a drop like that. I saw what happened to that vehicle. Its wreckage was scattered all over the place. That's a deep canyon. She's one mighty lucky young woman."

Then Jewel died. Tavia's heart pounded erratically as she turned her head away and began to cry anew, the sound echoing in her ears, and she felt sick to her stomach. *If there is a God, how could he take that beautiful girl who had so much to live for—and leave me?*

George Flint pulled his handkerchief from his pocket, removed his glasses and wiped at his eyes. "That she is, only we don't look at it as luck. We believe God left her here with us. Having her survive that terrible tragedy doesn't diminish the pain of losing our Adam, but it helps us cope with it a little better."

"I understand. If she, or anyone else, had been in that vehicle, the way it tumbled into that canyon, there is no doubt in my mind they would have perished, too. Just be glad she was thrown clear before it went over the guardrail or you would have been facing two funerals."

Jewel was in that truck when it went over the guardrail. Why haven't you found her body? If they'd take this thing out of my throat I could tell you!

"I'm glad they were able to bring your grandson's body up out of that canyon as quickly as they did, but it'll probably take a long time to get that SUV brought up with the kind of damage it sustained," the trooper said, keeping his voice low. "Most of it may never be brought up."

Grandpa turned his head away and blinked hard. "I'm glad, too. Since a number of folks will be coming from out of town, we've had to delay the funeral. We're all dreading it but we're thankful Adam's fiancée is still with us."

"Well, I'm here to check on another accident victim so I'll be going now. Please express my sympathy to Mr. and Mrs. Flint on the loss of their son."

The man stuck out his hand and Grandpa took it, giving it a vigorous shake. "Thanks for stopping by. I'll let my son and his wife know you were here."

George watched until the door closed behind the trooper, then turned his gaze to Tavia. "God must have a very special purpose for you, to spare your life like He did."

A special purpose for me? You've got to be kidding. If there was a God, He wouldn't care about a little nobody like me. Are you sure your God didn't make a mistake?

"That grandson of mine sure had good taste. He always told me he was saving himself until the right girl came along. Looks to me like his wait paid off. He got you!" After blotting his eyes with his handkerchief once more, George scooted a chair up close to the bed and lowered himself into it, leaning back and crossing his arms. "You ever go fishing, Jewel?"

Tavia blinked her eyes, unable to stop the flow of tears, knowing he was waiting for a response. *He's trying to change the subject to get my mind off Adam's death.*

"That a yes? Maybe I'll take you fishing when you feel up to it. Adam always liked to go fishing with me. The little tackle box I gave him when he was about eight is still out in the garage. I know a swell place to fish. You'll like it. At least, I think you will." He gave her a smile of satisfaction. "What am I saying? I know you'll like it. Adam loved it."

You're such a nice man, Mr. Flint.

"The place is surrounded by trees, and the water is so clear you can actually see the fish." He huffed. "Bet you couldn't do that in Tennessee. Isn't that where you indicated you're from?"

He gazed off in the distance and Tavia could tell the pleasant scene was playing out in his memory. "We'll wade out a ways and I'll teach you how to cast that line right into those fish's mouths!"

Becoming suddenly somber, the man placed his hand near Tavia's head. The past few days had taken their toll on him, too. "I'm glad you loved my grandson. I know he loved you," Grandpa went on, speaking with great effort. "You were all he could talk about when he came home for Christmas—bragged about you all the time. I'm sorry the two of you had such little time together, but I know you shared a great love."

He leaned back in the chair. "Once this ordeal is over and you're released from the hospital, I want to know everything about you, and about the time you and Adam had together. I want us to be friends, Jewel. If there's ever anything you need, you just ask ol' Grandpa."

Tavia's insides churned at his words. *I knew your grandson for a few minutes, that's all!*

Grandpa rose and patted Tavia's shoulder. "I think you've had enough excitement. You need to rest now. I'm going to ask the nurse to give you something to help you sleep. With all that's happened today, I'm sure you'll need it. I'll wait until you're asleep, then call my friend to pick me up."

She managed a slight nod. He gave her a smile, then moved out of the room, closing the door behind him. Her insides still thrashing about, Tavia took several breaths and tried to relax against the pillow, the news of Adam's death too much to bear.

As Grandpa had promised, the nurse came in and gave her something to help her relax and get some sleep. Tavia lay staring at the ceiling. Somehow, someway, she had to make them understand the truth.

Not realizing she'd finally drifted off to sleep, she awakened with a start when someone brushed against her arm.

"I didn't mean to disturb you," a nurse whispered as she checked the IV connection. "Try to go back to sleep."

Tavia shifted her position and glanced at the window. It was dark outside. Had she really been asleep that long?

"It's nearly eleven, time for my shift to end. The night nurse will be in later. Oh, your grandfather said, since you were sleeping, he was going on home and some of your family would be back first thing in the morning."

Tavia gave her a slight nod. Grandpa needed his rest, too. She was glad he'd gone home.

"I know you're uncomfortable but you're doing quite well. The doctor will be taking that tube out soon and you'll be able to talk to your family. Won't that be nice?"

Talk to them? A sudden chill ran through Tavia at the thought. *I've never actually told them I was Jewel. Surely they'll realize, even though I tried, I couldn't tell them with this tube going down my throat, or even write them a note with broken bones in my writing hand and an IV in my left hand.*

The woman smoothed Tavia's sheet. "I suppose they'll be taking you home soon. Patients always feel much better once they're back in their own beds. You'll be your old self in no time."

My own bed? I doubt I even have a bed anymore. My stuff has probably been hauled off to the city dump by now. I doubt my rotten landlord has kept anything for me. He probably sold it to make my back rent.

"You're lucky to have such a nice family," the woman went on as she moved to the nightstand and began neatly rearranging things. "Some patients never have anyone come to see them. Can you imagine being all alone like that, without any family at all? I sure can't."

Tavia struggled to get control of the tears that continued to well up in her eyes. What am I going to do? Where am I going to go?

"Jewel?"

She turned toward the whispered name and found James Flint standing in the doorway.

"It's rather late. Are you a relative?" the nurse asked, looking perturbed.

James moved in awkwardly. His hair was disheveled and he looked totally worn out. "I'm her fiancé's father. I know it's late, but I really need to talk to her. Alone."

The woman's face took on a pleasant smile. "Come on in. She's had a good nap. I'm sure she's happy to see you."

James waited until the nurse was out the door, then moved to Tavia's side, pulling a chair close to the bed. "I—

I had to come back and see you. You've been on my mind constantly since Annie and I left you this afternoon."

Tavia's heart constricted. *He's finally realized I'm not Jewel.*

"Annie and I have been so upset by the loss of our son, I'm not sure we've accurately conveyed our feelings about your survival. It's so hard to talk about this in front of Annie, but there are some things I thought you should know."

I never meant to deceive you, James! Honest, I didn't.

"Adam has been our life. When the news came that he'd—well, you know—I can't even bring myself to say the word." The distraught man's eyes filled with tears and he stopped speaking, momentarily lowering his head into his hands.

Tavia felt herself weeping, too. Life wasn't fair!

"Though our Adam dated a number of girls in high school and college, he never found that one special person, until he met you." The man smiled at her through misty eyes. "Sometimes Annie and I wondered if he'd ever marry."

Your son found that one special person, Mr. Flint—Jewel! It was obvious the two of them were perfect together.

"Annie and I so looked forward to having grandchildren. But, now—"

I'm so, so sorry, but there was nothing Adam could do.

"We came very close to losing Annie a number of

years ago." He choked back a sob, then rose and gently cupped Tavia's arm. "Though Annie hates it when I talk about it, she is still quite fragile. Among other health problems, her heart is very weak. That's why she reacted as she did today. She had to be hospitalized when they told her about the accident and that we'd lost Adam. For a few hours, they weren't sure she was going to make it."

He lifted his face toward the ceiling and drew a steadying breath, swallowing hard and blinking. Finally, after clearing his throat loudly, he continued, "I'm convinced that had you died in that accident along with Adam, Annie would have died, too. You're the only bright spot in our lives now, Jewel. The one thing that is keeping my wife alive. I love her with all my heart. If she was ever taken from me—"

A layer of tears clouded Tavia's vision. *I didn't know. Why are you telling me this? It makes things so much harder.*

"I—I just wanted to come and tell you this, to let you know how much you mean to us. Especially to Annie." His shoulders drooping, James leaned against the bed and stood staring at Tavia for a long time before saying anything. "I—I had another purpose in coming here. As Adam's father, you deserve to know."

Tavia lifted her brows in question. *What else could he possibly have to tell her that would upset him like this?*

"Tomorrow—" He paused and began wringing his hands, his face breaking out in a sweat. "Tomorrow morning—at ten—we're—we're burying our son. I know you'd like to be there, but—" He gestured toward the machines beeping away beside the bed. "But—the hospital told us it's not possible."

I don't have any right to be at Adam's funeral, except as a short-term friend, but I wish I could spare your family this pain.

He reached out his hand, gently touching her face. "I know how hard this must be on you, not being able to go."

His words, spoken with such love and compassion, shredded Tavia's heart to bits. Watching Adam's parents, seeing their anguish and knowing she was going to be responsible for hurting them further when they found out about Jewel, touched her more deeply than she'd ever been touched. She'd never witnessed true love before. No matter how long she lived, she'd always remember the love she'd seen in the Flint family. To Tavia, it was the kind of love you only read about in fiction, and how she longed to be a part of it.

"I have to get back to Annie. I don't want her waking up and finding me gone." He moved to the foot of the bed and stood facing Tavia, his hands plunged deep into his pockets. "Do—do you think you'll be all right? Would you like me to call a nurse to come in and stay with you for a while?"

With great effort, Tavia gave her head an obvious shake.

He paused in the doorway, one hand resting on the

frame. "We'll probably be here at the hospital by mid-afternoon. You're our number-one concern now, Jewel. Annie and I—and Grandpa, too—love you, and want to take care of you." He backed out the door, closing it quietly behind him.

Chapter Six

She spent a restless night. If she'd been able to toss and turn in the bed she would have, but the IV and the tube, not to mention the constant pain in her broken ribs and arm, made it impossible. The faces of James, Annie and Grandpa were constantly before her, like pictures hung on a wall. Especially Annie. No mother should have to lose her son.

A woman dressed in a business suit and holding a clipboard tapped on Tavia's partially opened door then stepped inside. "I'm from the hospital's admittance office. I need to get some information from you. Since you were unconscious when they brought you in, we were unable to ask about your insurance. You do have insurance coverage, don't you?"

Her heart pounding, Tavia shook her head.

The woman made a notation on the clipboard. "I'm

sure there was adequate accident coverage on the vehicles involved to cover any hospital bills you might incur, but we like to have this information for our records." With a smile, she turned and moved toward the door. "Thank you. That's really all I needed to know."

The morning dragged on, with Tavia continually watching the clock. At ten, she burst into tears. Just knowing those who loved Adam were gathered together at the church for his funeral made her heart feel it was being crushed by some unseen weight. She could visualize the family huddled together on one of the pews as the organ played and the preacher said a few words, probably reading from the Bible. She glanced toward the beautiful bouquet the Flints had sent her, and the small vase of white daisies, and wondered how many baskets of flowers graced the front of the sanctuary. Was the church filled to capacity with their many friends and business associates? She wished she could be there to pay her respects. As who? Jewel? Or as Tavia—the imposter?

I am an imposter, she told herself. If only I could tell them.

These people have been kind to me, treated me with more love and respect than anyone I've ever known. But any minute now, the clock will strike midnight, the truth will come out, and I'll become Tavia McRae again. A poor little girl with no money, no job and no place to go.

The doctor came in a bit later and, after looking over

her chart and checking her head wounds and her arm, and talking about her broken ribs, said, "We'll be able to remove that tube from your throat soon. You may not have noticed, but we've been gradually decreasing some of the settings now that you are doing most of the work on your own. You just might get rid of that thing tomorrow."

While Tavia would be glad to have that uncomfortable tube removed, she also knew it would be her day of reckoning. With it gone, there would no longer be a reason for her not to tell the Flint family who she was.

A selfish thought came to her. Since no one questioned the fact that she was Jewel, could she possibly mask herself as Jewel a little longer? Just until she was able to take care of herself and Annie's health improved? Tavia shuddered at the ridiculous idea. Only someone desperate would do such a cruel thing. But—wasn't she desperate?

Grandpa came into her room later, explaining the funeral had been exceptionally hard on both Annie and James, and he'd encouraged them to go on home and rest, volunteering to come to the hospital in their place. "I'm sure they'll be here this evening," he told her, scooting a chair up close. "I told them you'd understand."

Tavia nodded. She wanted only the best for them. Though she'd known them for only a short time, she'd grown to respect them both. Why couldn't she have been born into a family like Adam's?

Beck's smiling face appeared in the partially opened doorway. "Hi, I hope I'm not disturbing you."

Grandpa turned at the sound of his voice. "Of course you're not disturbing us. Come on in."

He's walking!

Beck hobbled into the room with the assistance of a cane. "How is Annie doing? At times, she didn't look like she'd make it through the service."

Grandpa shrugged. "James took her home. I think the doc gave her something to make her rest. She didn't sleep at all last night. He found her lying in Adam's bed, his picture cuddled to her breast. It's like she's in a fog. It seems to take every ounce of her strength just to get dressed."

"How is—" Speaking in soft tones, he nodded his head toward the bed "—she?"

"Hard to tell since she can't talk, but she seems to be doing as well as can be expected. The doc told us he might take the tube out tomorrow."

Leaning on his cane, Beck rounded the bed and stood staring at Tavia, his eyes kind and filled with concern.

Grandpa rose and motioned toward his chair. "If you're going to be here for a few minutes, Beck, why don't you sit down? I think I'll go out to the vending machines and get a soft drink. Can I get you anything?"

"No, thank you, sir." Beck shuffled a few steps then, holding on to the arms of the chair, lowered himself and sat down, his broken leg extended out in front of him. "I had a cup of coffee in my room." He smiled up at her. "I hope you're doing okay, ma'am, and feeling some better."

She blinked her eyes in response.

He fidgeted in the seat, glancing away from her face and toward the window. "It's kinda strange, talking to someone who can't answer back. I—I don't know exactly what to say."

I don't care what you say—just keep talking.

"Umm, let me see." He allowed a small smile to curl at the corners of his mouth. "Are you a sports fan? We could talk football."

She gave a miniscule shake of her head.

He twisted his mouth to one side and frowned. "I'm not much on current events or politics."

Again, she shook her head.

"Oh, so you aren't, either. Gardening? Sewing? The latest fashions? I'm sure not up on those subjects."

She raised her brows and gave a slight nod toward him.

He smiled up at her. "You wanna hear about me?"

I live a pretty boring life. I've never been married— or divorced. I don't believe in divorce. When a man and woman take marriage vows, it should be for life. That's not just my way of looking at it, it's God's way.

It surprised her that a nice-looking man like Beck would remain single. He had to be in his late-twenties, maybe even thirty.

"I nearly got married. Once," he went on. "It's a long story. Maybe I'll tell you about it sometime. What else do you want to know? I doubt you would want to hear about the trucking business. It's about all I know."

Tavia widened her eyes and nodded, hoping he'd continue.

Beck grinned. "You really want to hear about the trucking business?"

Again, she nodded.

He used his hands to lift his bad leg and adjust its position. "You sure about this? Okay, you asked for it. The trucking business. I worked on a loading dock when I was in high school and found I liked being around trucks. The week after my eighteenth birthday, I enrolled in the truck driver's class at the local vocational-technical training center, got my license and began doing short hauls around the Denver area. About a year later, I went to work for one of the cross-country lines, found I liked those longer runs, and began saving toward buying my own truck. Three years later I bought one." He chuckled. "It looked like an old clunker, but mechanically, it was in great shape. Drove it for about four years, then bought the truck that—" He stopped midsentence, clamping his lips together and lowering his gaze to the floor.

Tavia felt a shudder course through her body. The truck that caused the accident!

After several tense moments, Beck pulled his handkerchief from his pocket and blew his nose. "I'm sorry, Jewel. That was careless of me. I didn't mean to remind you of your loss. Please forgive me."

"Can you believe that machine ate my dollar bill?"

Grandpa swept into the room shaking his head. "Guess I should've gone to the nurses' station and complained, but I didn't." The man stopped in his tracks. "What's going on here? You look like you've been suckin' on persimmons."

Beck braced himself with his cane and pulled to a standing position. "I put my foot in my mouth." He hobbled toward the door, pausing by Grandpa to add, "Maybe I'd better be going."

Grandpa looked from Beck to Tavia and back again. "Think you can make it back to your room by yourself?"

Beck managed a smile. "Yes, sir. I think I can. I got here by myself."

The two men shook hands, then Beck turned back to face Tavia. "I'm sorry. I didn't mean to bring up unpleasant things. I hope you know that."

Tavia bobbed her head. I'm so glad you came, Beck.

As soon as he was out the door, Grandpa seated himself and rested his elbows on her bed. "Now, where were we?"

Beck paused outside the door and switched his cane to his other hand. His sole purpose for coming to Jewel's room had been to cheer her up. He could only imagine what the day must have been like for her, knowing her fiancé was being lowered into his grave. She'd been upset, as he'd known she'd be, but she seemed to be taking it a little better than he'd expected. Probably, with her own physical problems and the meds they were giving her to take the edge off her pain, the reality of his death hadn't fully hit her yet. But once she got out of the hospital and Adam was no longer in her life, it'd jolt her pretty hard.

Chapter Seven

Annie arrived that evening looking as though the angel of death was hovering over her shoulder as she clung to her husband's arm. She was still dressed in black, and her eyes were partially hidden by the big brim of her hat and so swollen you could barely make out her pupils when James ushered her into Tavia's room. James, too, looked haggard and old. There were lines etched on his face and wrinkles beside his eyes that Tavia had never noticed before.

He ushered his wife to the chair beside Tavia's bed and assisted her into the seat. "I tried to get her to stay home, but she was concerned about you."

Annie, you shouldn't have come. Today must have been a horrible day for you.

"I—I had to see you—to hold your hand. To—to know you're still with us, Jewel. Seeing you like this, and touching you, is a little like having a small piece of my son still here." Annie tightly cupped her frail hand around Tavia's arm. "You have to promise you'll never leave us. Please. Promise me that!"

I can't make a promise like that. You'll hate me when you find out I'm not Jewel.

James moved up beside his wife's chair, resting his hand on her shoulder. "Annie and I have thoroughly discussed it. We want you to come and live with us. There really isn't anything to keep you in California now, with—with Adam gone. Adam told us you'd quit your job and were looking for another apartment. We want to take you home with us, Jewel, as soon as the doctor releases you. Then when you're well, if you decide you still want to stay with us, we'll all go to California, get yours and Adam's things and sell his condo."

Overwhelmed by their kind offer, Tavia managed a slight smile—until she remembered they were inviting Jewel, their son's fiancée, to come and live with them. Not Tavia, the deceiver. She couldn't take advantage of their generous offer. It wouldn't be fair to them. Yet, how could she tell them no, without telling them that somewhere, down deep in that canyon, lay the real Jewel? Dead. And—if she were able to tell them—could either of them survive the shock of another loss?

Annie smiled at Tavia through her tears. "You will come home with us? Let us take care of you, won't you, Jewel?"

The moment had come. Annie had asked her a direct question. Tavia stared into the reddened eyes and the tear-stained face. This woman had buried her only son that very day. Could she add to her grief by refusing her offer?

James leaned over his wife's shoulder, cupping his hand over hers as it rested on Tavia's arm. "Please say yes, Jewel. It would mean so much to Annie and me to have you in our home."

Tavia stared up at these two people who had come to mean so much to her.

Annie's grip tightened on her arm. "Jewel, you are going to come home with us, aren't you?"

I have to answer. I can't stall any longer.

"Just give us a nod, or blink or something." Annie's eyes were pleading.

I hate myself for what I am about to do, but I have no other place to go. And I can't add to this woman's hurt. Not until she's stronger. Blinking back tears of guilt and anguish, Tavia nodded.

Immediately, Annie's expression brightened. "Oh, Jewel, I can't tell you how happy this makes me! Your place is with us now. Just like Ruth's place was with Naomi. We're your family."

Ruth? Naomi? Who are they?

"I've always loved that story in the Bible," Annie went on, her trembling hand still holding on to Tavia's arm, her tears falling softly onto the bedspread. "The way Ruth stayed with her mother-in-law, Naomi, when her husband died." She gave Tavia a sweet smile. "I want us to be as close as Naomi and Ruth were. Theirs was such a precious relationship."

Oh, Bible characters. No wonder I didn't know who those women were.

"I'm glad you're going to move in with us. Annie was so afraid you'd say no." James tugged on his wife's arm, pulling her close to him. "But, right now, both you girls need your rest. I think it's time for me to take my wife home. Before long, Jewel, I'll be taking you home, too. Maybe as early as tomorrow."

After a fairly restful night's sleep, thanks to the medication the nurse had given her at Dr. Stevens's order, Tavia awoke to a beautiful sunny morning and found Annie seated in a chair next to her bed, her eyes ringed with dark circles from lack of sleep.

The pain in Tavia's ribs was nearly unbearable, but she didn't want to let on in front of Annie. Even the tiniest movement made her want to scream out. Would this constant pain ever end?

"I hope I didn't awaken you. I couldn't sleep last night. I kept thinking of you lying in this hospital bed thinking about Adam. I know you miss him. I wish we hadn't had to tell you about him, but you had to know."

Tavia gave her head a slight shake. Dr. Stevens had said he'd probably remove the tube from her throat today. Without that tube, all of the reasons for her not being able to talk would vanish and, unless she lied outright, her deception would be discovered.

Annie rose and leaned over her. "You're trembling? Are you cold? Do you want another blanket?"

Tavia shook her head.

"You're as beautiful as I knew you'd be, though from Adam's description of you I thought perhaps your hair might be a bit darker." She huffed. "But, that's a man for you." Annie brushed a lock of hair from Tavia's forehead.

The smile left Annie's pale face and her eyes thinned, as if she had something else on her mind. "I—I don't know exactly how to put this." Annie paused, obviously weighing her words carefully. "But—since you and Adam decided to get engaged before his graduation, I was wondering if—" She closed her eyes and swallowed hard. "If—you—are pregnant?"

Tavia gave her head a violent shake. Those were the very words she had asked Jewel.

"Please don't be mad at me. I didn't want to ask you in front of James and Grandpa. My question wasn't meant to condemn. I only asked—because of the accident. The doctor never mentioned a pregnancy. I thought—maybe you had, in some way, communicated with him, asking him not to mention it to us since you and Adam weren't married yet."

Again, Tavia shook her head.

"Actually, as long as the accident hadn't injured the

baby, I would have been thrilled to learn you were pregnant. A baby would be like having a bit of my precious son still with us." Tears began to stream down Annie's cheeks. "Please don't be upset with me for asking. I hope you understand."

Tavia did everything she could to communicate with Annie that she wasn't upset by her question.

"Did Adam ever tell you we nearly lost him at birth?"

Tavia shook her head.

"Due to my poor health, the doctor said we shouldn't even try to have a baby, but I couldn't imagine going through life without being a mother. James was against it, too, because he was worried about losing me. But God had other plans and blessed us with Adam. Knowing he was a miracle child made him even more special to us." Annie sniffled.

Her words went like an arrow through Tavia's heart. Oh, Annie, and now you've lost him.

Dr. Stevens entered the room accompanied by an intern, Tavia's chart in hand. He smiled at his patient. "Well, according to the good report I see on your chart, I'd say it's time for that tube to go."

Annie's elation was uncontainable. "This is so exciting. Does this mean she'll be ready to go home tomorrow?"

"If everything looks as good in the morning as it does now!" He bent over Tavia, examining the area where he'd removed the stitches from the gash on her forehead. "Her head looks good and shouldn't give her any more trouble, but her throat will be pretty tender for a few days. She should stick with mostly liquids until it gets to feeling better."

Annie brightened. "Oh, James will be so pleased. I promise we'll take good care of her."

Dr. Stevens gently lifted one of Tavia's eyelids, then the other, peering into their depths with his small flashlight. "Good responses. I'd say you're on your way to a full recovery—it's just going to take time. After I finish making rounds," he said, placing the flashlight back into his pocket, "we'll remove that tube."

Tavia stared at him, aghast at his words, even though she'd expected them.

"Actually," the doctor went on, "it may be a day or two before you can carry on a complete conversation. Just whisper, and don't push it beyond its limits."

Tavia nodded, glad for at least a few hours' reprieve. Anything to delay the inevitable.

Dr. Stevens looped his stethoscope about his neck and smiled at his patient as he headed for the door. "I'll be back."

Annie clapped her hands with joy. "Jewel, it's going to be so wonderful to be able to talk with you. There's so much I want to know about you and my son."

Wonderful? If I tell you the truth, it won't be wonderful. The truth may destroy you.

"James and I want to hear every little detail about the

time you spent with our darling Adam. How you met. The places you went together."

Tavia winced at Annie's words. *Only the real Jewel could tell you those things, dear Annie. The only details I know are the ones Jewel and Adam told me, and that wasn't much.*

Annie glanced at her watch. "I'd better be going. James insisted I catch a little nap before he comes home from his office. We'll both be up to see you tonight." She gave Tavia's arm a gentle pat. "Just think. By this time, tomorrow, you'll be home with us, where you belong."

Only if I decide to go through with this charade for a few more days. Until you're stronger, and I can figure out what I can do to take care of myself.

Annie gave her a wave and disappeared.

A severe pain shot through Tavia's right side as she lifted her hips to adjust her position. With her broken ribs, there seemed to be no way to get comfortable.

A half hour later, Dr. Stevens came bustling into her room, followed by an intern and a nurse. After giving Tavia a pleasant smile, he nodded to the intern who quickly removed the IV from her arm. Just the simple act of scratching her nose unencumbered was exhilarating.

The doctor circled her hand with his and gently began to massage the IV intersection area with his thumb. At his direction, the nurse checked Tavia's vital signs and, after checking the oximeter for her breathing capacity, gave him a nod of approval.

"We're going to suction this tube one more time before we remove it, Jewel," he explained. "Then I'll deflate the little balloon holding it in place and take it out. It won't be painful, but it will be uncomfortable. Bear with me, okay?"

She stared up into the doctor's face as he leaned over her, afraid to make even the tiniest movement. To her surprise, the tube came out more easily than she'd expected, but she felt herself gagging, and the gag turned into a coughing spell—each gulp for air digging at the sides of her burning throat, making her want to scream out as she struggled for breath. But soon, the coughing and gagging subsided and she was breathing totally on her own and, despite the terrible rawness in her throat, it felt good.

"You okay?"

Her hand rose to cup her throat as she gave him a nod.

"Don't try to talk until you feel like it. We'll use these nasal prongs for a little while to deliver some oxygen to those lungs of yours, just to be on the safe side. Everyone has a different degree of soreness from the tube. Some have very little, some more. It might be easier just to whisper. As to foods, you can eat whatever you want, but I'd keep it soft. And yes, you can go home tomorrow if you appear to be stable. You're one of the lucky ones. You have people who love you, and are willing to nurse you back to health. Not everyone is that fortunate."

His word hit Tavia with more force than whatever had broken her ribs. *I have to let them continue to believe I'm Jewel. At least, for a while. There's no other choice. And poor Annie can't take much more.*

"It's going to take some time for you to heal completely. A few days for your throat, but I doubt that cut on your head will give you any more grief. In a week or so, the pain from your fractured ribs should begin to subside, but I'm afraid you're going to have to wear that cast on your arm for at least another four or five weeks."

How can I get a job waitressing with a cast on my hand? Who'd want to hire me anyway? I don't have a permanent address or phone number to put on a résumé. How will I support myself until I'm well enough to work? Even if I apply for unemployment benefits, there'll be a waiting period.

"I've prescribed something for pain but I'm hoping you won't need it." Dr. Stevens headed for the door, followed by the intern and the nurse. "Try to get some rest. I'll see you in the morning." He hesitated in the doorway, one hand on the frame, bracing himself. "I'm not only the Flints' doctor, I'm their friend. All the love Annie has had for her son, she's transferred to you. Treat her kindly. She's been so depressed since Adam's death, if it weren't for you and James, she probably would have given up." He gave her a salute. "Didn't mean to leave you on such a sad note, but I thought you deserved to know."

Tavia watched him go, his words about Annie echoing through her mind, giving her even more reason to carry on with the deception that had been forced upon her. Once the door had closed behind him, she tried her voice. Though it was weak and it hurt, she was able to say, "Now what do I do?"

She stared at the ceiling for a long time, running things over and over in her mind. She hated this deception. Though she'd done many things in her life she'd been ashamed of, lying hadn't been one of them.

Tavia lifted her head slightly when she heard a noise in the hall.

Beck moved in through the door, maneuvering his cane even better than he had the last time he visited her. "Hey, you're making progress! You've got that tube out of your throat. Can you talk yet?"

Tavia shook her head and smiled at him, cradling her throat. It felt good to be able to smile without the restraint of the tube.

He crossed the floor slowly, his big grin never leaving as he cradled both an oversize yellow plush teddy bear and a bouquet of brilliant yellow daffodils in his free hand. "I guess it's kinda silly, buying a teddy bear for a grown woman, but I thought he might cheer you up."

It was all Tavia could do to keep from audibly thanking the thoughtful man. But, instead of trying to voice her thanks and letting anyone know she could talk, she simply smiled and mouthed the word.

"My mom always had daffodils growing around our porch when I was a kid. I can even remember times when they poked their heads through the snow."

She reached out her hand, now freed from the IV and pointed to an empty vase on the window sill.

"Want me to put these in that vase?"

She nodded, then reached out her hand toward the teddy bear.

"Want to hold him?"

She whispered a faint, "Yes."

"You can whisper now? Don't do it if it hurts." Beck placed the bear on the pillow next to her, then circled the bed, used her water pitcher to fill the vase, and placed it on her nightstand. "I—I don't know much about flowers, but I thought these were real pretty."

She waited until he glanced her way, then smiled and bobbed her head.

He moved into the empty chair beside her bed and sat watching her as she hugged the bear to her breast. "I'm glad you like him. He's my farewell gift. The doctor has released me."

Tavia lifted her brows in question. She couldn't imagine this being her last visit with Beck, and it made her sad. Other than Adam and his father, and Grandpa, of course, he was the nicest man she'd ever met. She loved being in his presence.

"Where am I going? Is that what you want to know?"

He hooked the handle of his cane on the arm of the chair and leaned forward, clasping his hands together and propping them on the edge of the mattress. "A friend of mine, another driver, has a little cabin up by Nederland, not too far from the Flints' home. He stopped by the hospital to see me the other day, and when I told him I didn't want to go back to my one-room apartment in Denver until I finished up with my physical therapy here at the hospital, he offered to let me stay there. I keep most of my clothes in the sleeper compartment of my truck and, thankfully, someone was good enough to retrieve them when it went off the road and hit that rocky hill. I have most of what I need. The rest the guy offered to get for me on his next run into Denver."

You're going to be staying nearby?

"Besides, I owe a great debt to both you and the Flints. I wasn't kidding when I said I would spend the rest of my life trying to make it up to all of you. I don't know exactly how, but I aim to do it."

Make things up to me? You certainly don't owe me anything. If you knew I was about to continue my deception you'd hate me.

"I'm hoping maybe Dr. Flint has some handyman jobs I can do for him. I'm a pretty good carpenter."

Tavia pointed toward his leg.

"My leg? It's doing okay. They say with physical therapy, it'll be back to normal within a few months."

She pointed to his head.

"It's doing okay, too. In fact, I've nearly forgotten about it. Your head doing okay?"

Tavia nodded. "Fine."

"Guess we were both pretty lucky to make it out alive. Poor Adam—" Beck swallowed hard enough that Tavia could see his Adam's apple rise and fall. "I wish I could have met him."

I wish you could have, too. You should have seen the loving way he treated Jewel.

"He was," she whispered softly.

"I've heard so many stories about him from the Flints."

I'd love to hear more about Adam. He was so kind to me.

"One, I especially remember." Beck laughed and slapped his knee. "One of Adam's friends was staying the weekend with him, and the two boys got into a pillow fight. Adam's friend's pillow ripped open and feathers went flying everywhere. Not to be outdone, Adam took a pair of scissors and cut his pillow open. By the time Annie came into the room to see what all the laughter and noise was about, the entire room was covered with feathers." Beck let out a chuckle. "I can just imagine the look on Annie's face when she opened that door."

I love to hear you laugh, Beck.

"Annie said the boys were sure they were in big trouble, but instead of being mad and getting after them, Annie walked right into the middle of the room, scooped up a couple of handfuls of the feathers and tossed them into the air. Before long, she was as covered with feathers as they were. I love that kind of woman. She knew how to enjoy her son. What memories he must have had."

I wish my mother had lived. If she'd been around things would have been different.

"I had great parents, but they were so busy working and trying to keep food on the table, they never seemed to have time for fun." Beck became somber. "Now, Adam's gone."

Tavia nodded. Why do bad things have to happen to such good people?

"Good thing Annie and James know the Lord. At least, they have hope. They know they'll see their son again someday."

Hope? You call that hope? Thinking there is a God up there who has this glorious place called heaven floating around on a cloud? And Adam is there? I don't call that hope. I call it wishful thinking.

"Hey, Beck. I was hoping I'd get here before you left. James told me they were releasing you today."

Tavia smiled. She'd recognize that voice anywhere. Grandpa.

The old man bent and poked a finger at the big bear's stomach. "Who is this guy? Never met him before."

Beck dipped his head shyly. "I brought him. I thought Jewel would enjoy his company."

"Good idea. I'll just bet she will." Grandpa's face

boasted a teasing smile. "Nice to see you, son. Hope that leg is doing okay."

"It's coming along real good, sir." Beck rose and offered his chair.

"Sit yourself back down. I wanna visit with this pretty little lady." Grandpa moved past Beck and bent over Tavia, giving her a big kiss on her cheek. "How's my girl today? Annie told me they were going to remove the tube. Feel better without it?"

Tavia whispered a soft, "Yes," then cupped her throat at the pain.

"Sore, huh? Well, don't rush it. Maybe by tomorrow some of that soreness will go away and you'll be able to speak without it hurting so much. Annie is really eager to get you home. She's had the housekeeper working in Adam's room, getting it ready for you. They'd better release you tomorrow, or they're going to have one very unhappy woman on their hands. James and I have had to laugh at the way she's making sure every little thing is just right, but it's good for her to have something to do besides grieve for Adam."

Beck frowned. "I hope she's not overdoing it."

"The housekeeper is doing the work. Annie's just giving the orders." He motioned toward Beck. "I hear you're going to be staying at a friend's house for the time being."

"Yes, sir. I'm taking a medical leave of absence while I heal and a friend offered to let me stay in his cabin.

It's not far from here." Beck lowered his eyes and fiddled with the handle of his cane. "Before I go back to driving, the company I work for insisted I get some counseling, considering what happened. I guess that's standard for any truck driver who—" He let his words trail off without finishing his sentence.

Grandpa placed a reassuring hand on his shoulder. "Sounds like good advice to me."

"I try not to say too much about it, since I didn't lose a loved one like all of you did, but I have nightmares nearly every night about the accident."

Grandpa pulled off his glasses and stuck them in his pocket. "Beck, you've got to stop that. No one is blaming you. Not me, not Adam's parents, and I'm sure Jewel doesn't blame you, either."

Grandpa nodded and smiled fondly at Tavia. "Praise God, she's right here with us still and will soon be going home with us. Annie and James and I want you to know you are welcome to visit Jewel at their home anytime you like."

"Thank you, sir. I was hoping they'd feel that way. I really need to check on her, at least until I know she's well enough to go on with her life."

Early that evening, Annie showed up at the hospital with Grandpa by her side. Annie's face actually had a little bit of color to it.

"I'm so pleased you got that awful tube out of your throat. As soon as you're able, I want to hear everything about you," she said, clasping her hands about Tavia's.

She turned quickly and, spotting the yellow teddy bear, bent to pat him. "Where did this cute guy come from? He's adorable."

Tavia cuddled the bear in her arm and whispered, "Beck." *It was so sweet of him to get me such a beautiful bear.*

"I can't tell you how happy it makes me to know you'll be going home with us."

I'm feeling worse about this by the minute. I'm still not sure I can do this to you.

"By the way," Annie went on, her expression suddenly changing. "The hospital gave James a bag with your clothing and shoes in it. I doubt they're worth keeping since they probably have blood all over them, but I didn't want to throw them away without your permission. I put it in the laundry room. You can go through the bag when you feel up to it."

Tavia's mind raced. *What was I wearing? Oh, yes. Jeans, a print shirt and a pair of white tennis shoes. Did I have anything in the pockets? Anything that would identify me? Sometimes I put my key ring and my lipstick in my pocket. That key ring has that little identification tag attached to it. Did I put it in my pocket that day?* She gave an audible gasp. *I'm not sure! What if Annie decides to go through the pockets? Oh, dear, how can I even think about going through with this farce?*

"Jewel, are you cold?"

Tavia shook her head.

"Did I upset you with all this talk about your clothing?" Annie gave a slight shrug. "Maybe I should just go ahead and throw those things away. I'm sure they're not wearable."

Tavia's heartbeat quickened as she whispered the words, "No. Keep." *If I did have my key ring in my pocket, it might fall out if you were to take those things out of the bag.*

"Oh, Jewel. I'm sorry. I know your throat must hurt terribly and here I am, asking you all sorts of questions."

Tavia sucked in a deep breath and nodded.

"Okay, I won't throw them away."

Tavia forced a smile, feeling better that the bag wouldn't be opened until she could get her hands on it, then asked, "James?"

Annie linked her fingers with Tavia's. "James? You want to know where James is?"

"I'm right here." James strode into the room and hurried to Tavia's side. "I had to stop on the way into the hospital and see how one of my patients is doing. He's getting along fine. He's going home tomorrow, too."

"Look, James! No tubes!" Annie proudly pointed toward Tavia. "Isn't that wonderful? And they've removed her IV, too."

James's brows raised as he gazed at Tavia. "Yes, indeed, that is wonderful." He sent a smile toward the teddy bear. "Did you bring that, Annie?"

"No, Beck did. Wasn't that thoughtful of him?"

"Yeah, why didn't I think of doing something nice like that?"

Annie stood on tiptoes and kissed her husband's cheek. "You, my sweet husband, do so many thoughtful things for all of us."

James pulled Annie close and nuzzled his chin in her hair. "You are the most important thing in the world to me. If I lost you, I don't know what I'd do with myself."

Though James was smiling and laughing when he made that remark, Tavia knew he meant it. Annie was his life. He'd made that perfectly clear a number of times.

"Well, tomorrow is going to be a busy day. We want Jewel rested and perky when Dr. Stevens comes in to check her out in the morning. I suggest we get out of here and let her get to sleep." James relaxed his hold on his wife and leaning over Tavia, gave her a warm smile. "Our home is your home now, Jewel. You have no idea what it means to us to be able to share it with you." He bent and kissed her cheek. "Good night, sleep tight."

Annie slid close to him and leaned her head against his shoulder. "We love you, Jewel. You're our daughter now. We'll be here bright and early to take you home."

Tavia whispered, "Good night." Just the thought of tomorrow and its activities struck fear into her heart. I have to do this. It's not only myself I'm concerned about, it's Annie, too. I have to let them think I'm Jewel, at least a little bit longer, until Annie has had time to adjust to the loss of her son.

With the nurse's help Tavia made her way to the little bathroom and washed her face and brushed her teeth. It felt good to be able to move around again without being anchored to a machine or the IV. Bracing her hands on the sink, she stared into the mirror. *Do I look like my mother? She couldn't have been much older than me when she died. I wish I could remember her. I wish my dad had talked more about her. Surely she loved me like Annie loved Adam. I wonder if she held me in her arms and rocked me like some of the mothers I see in the movies. Did my dad start drinking because he lost her? There's so much I'd like to know about my parents.*

Forget your parents. Concentrate! You have to decide what you're going to do tomorrow when Adam's parents come for you. You have two choices. You can go home peaceably with the Flints and stay with them until you are able to take care of yourself and get a job. Perhaps by then, Annie will be better able to cope with the truth. You can always repay them for their expenses, although it may take you years.

Closing her eyes, she tried to block out anything that would keep her from the decision that must be made.

Or when the Flints come for you, you can tell them the whole ugly truth. Try to convince them you never meant to deceive them, but due to your circumstances there was no way you could explain what had actually happened. By the time you figured things out, there was Annie's fragile heart condition to deal with. She was too weak to take the news that she'd lost Jewel, too.

Tavia felt a tear roll down her cheek. Just the thought of Annie collapsing and going into cardiac arrest made her weep. The woman had been so good to her. Would it really hurt that much to put off telling them the truth for a few more days? A few weeks, at the most?

And what about her? What would become of her if the truth were to come out? If she told the Flints, they wouldn't pay for her medical bills when she was released, and there was no way she could pay them. And where could she go? No, there was no one to help her out—except the Flints. But did her own needs justify lying and taking advantage of their generosity?

There really wasn't a choice. She had to go through with it.

"Feel like trying to drink a little juice?" the nurse asked her the next morning as she came smiling into her room.

Tavia glanced at the breakfast tray. After not eating real food for several days, even the bland-looking applesauce, something she rarely ate, looked good. But, unfortunately, it didn't slide past her raw throat as easily as she'd hoped.

Dr. Stevens came in shortly after she'd finished eating, clipboard in hand and wearing his usual pleasant smile. "Well, from the looks of things, I'd say you're ready to go home. How are the ribs doing?"

She frowned. "Sore."

"Sorry, I know how you're hurting, but there's not much we can do for those ribs except give them time to heal. Sometimes, taking a soft bath towel and pinning it securely around your ribcage helps. You might give it a try when you get home. The nurse tells me your throat is still quite sore. That's to be expected. Just go easy on it, give it a day or two and it should be back to normal. Overall, considering your injuries, you've done quite well."

"Thank you." Tavia was surprised the words came out as easily as they did. "You've—been—very—nice."

"I'm sure the Flints will be here soon. I've signed your release papers and James has taken care of your bill. You're ready to go. Any questions?"

She pointed to the cast. "How—long?"

"Let's plan on about four to six weeks. I know that sounds like a long time, but it won't be that bad. We want to make sure that wrist is healed before we get rid of that cast. Anything else?"

Tavia shook her head.

"Fine. You've been a good patient. I'll need to see you in a few days to take those stitches out. Have Annie call and set up your appointment."

Tavia nodded and returned his smile as he moved out the door. What was he going to think of her when the truth came out?

She froze as the door was pushed open and Annie and James Flint rushed into her room.

"We ran into Dr. Stevens in the hall. He said you were doing fine," Annie said excitedly, bending over Tavia and planting a kiss on her forehead.

James took Tavia's good hand in his and smiled down at her. "Are you ready to go home, Jewel?"

Tavia's startled gaze went from one to the other, her heart pounding erratically.

Chapter Eight

Beck cast a quick look at his wristwatch. Surely by now the Flints were at the hospital getting Jewel released.

He picked up his nearly cold cup of coffee and stared into it. The little cabin his friend had loaned him was exactly that—a cabin—but it met his needs and he was grateful for it. He had water, the cookstove worked, there was a microwave and refrigerator, a toaster, a telephone and plenty of firewood cut and stacked by the door. There was even a CD player and an old television set with a roof-mounted antenna, but the picture wasn't too good. He'd had a rental car delivered to the hospital when he'd been released, and he'd stopped by the grocery store to stock up on supplies, so he had everything he really needed. When he got a chance, he'd pick up a few CDs, but for now, his choices were radio or snowy TV pictures.

"I wonder how Jewel is doing?" he asked aloud, laughing at himself. "Living alone and spending most of your life behind the steering wheel of a truck makes a guy talk to himself." He stared out the window at the beautiful Rocky Mountains, a scene he never tired of seeing. "She sure is pretty. I can see why the Flints went after her."

Shrugging, he placed his cup on the scuffed-up end table beside his chair. "Should have been me instead of him. *Lord, why you took that young man and left me behind, I'll never figure out. And why did Jewel have to get hurt? None of this makes any sense to me at all, Lord. Pardon my questioning of Your wisdom, I mean no disrespect, but I just don't get it!"*

Beck put a hand on the phone, lifted it, then placed it back in its cradle. Even if he called, the hospital probably wouldn't give him any information, but he'd sure like to know if she was being released today. Maybe he'd phone the Flint house later and ask. Yes, that's what he'd do. He'd give the Flints a call.

Closing her eyes for one brief moment, Tavia called out from deep within herself. *God! If You are real, forgive me for what I am about to do.*

"Jewel, are you okay?"

She opened her eyes to find Annie hovering over her, her eyes wide with concern.

"I'm—fine," she managed to say.

"Then you're ready to go?" James asked, stepping up beside his wife.

Tavia swallowed at the lump in her throat. With great effort and a heavy heart, she nodded her head and murmured a weak, "Yes, I'm ready."

"I've brought you a coat and a small bag for your nightgown and toiletries." Annie scurried about the room, pulling things out of the drawers and placing them in the bag. "James can carry your flowers. He's already pulled the car up under the canopy." Annie glanced about the room. "I think that's everything."

Tavia felt sick to her stomach. She worried about the questions to come at the Flints'. Questions for which she had no answers. After all, she knew very little about Adam and not much more about Jewel.

"One thing before we leave!" Annie reached for Tavia's left hand and cradled it lovingly. "I've brought your engagement ring. I know Adam would want you to have it."

Tavia felt her heart clench. That ring had changed her life.

Annie carefully slipped the ring onto the third finger of Tavia's left hand, then stepped back to admire it. "It's perfect on you. I can't tell you the joy I feel just seeing it there."

The sight of that ring on her finger made Tavia hold her breath as visions of the beautiful, smiling Jewel Mallory pulling off her ring and handing it over the seat to her, begging her to try it on, came flooding back. If it wasn't for that ring being on her hand at the time of the accident, and everyone assuming she was Jewel because of it, things would certainly have turned out differently. Instead of staying in a private room at a first-class hospital and heading for the Flints' lovely home, she'd have been sent to a ward in the County Hospital, then she'd have had to go to the local rescue mission, begging for help. And she would have never met Annie and James and Beck, and fallen in love with each of them.

Annie pulled a tissue from the box on the nightstand and gently wiped the tears from Tavia's cheeks. "I'm sorry, sweetie, I didn't mean to make you cry. Maybe I shouldn't have brought that ring to you this morning. You've been through so much, but I just knew you'd want to have it back."

I haven't been through nearly as much as you, Annie!

Annie cupped Tavia's ringed hand in hers. "I can't begin to tell you what this means to me. I'm so pleased you're going home with us. I just knew Adam's fiancée would want to be with his family at a time like this."

"Here's your chariot!"

Tavia spun her head toward the voice as an orderly moved into the room, pushing a wheelchair. He rolled it up beside the bed and waited.

James latched on to his wife's arm. "Are you girls going to talk all day, or are we going to take Jewel home?"

Annie smiled up into his face. "Let's get her home. We'll have plenty of time to talk later."

As Tavia was assisted from the bed and into the wheelchair, a heaviness settled over her. These kind people deserved to know the truth. But one look at the joy on Annie's face was all it took to make her decide to keep her silence. At least for a while longer.

As the chair was rolled toward the door, Tavia took one last look at the bed she'd vacated. Once she left that hospital, she would no longer be Tavia MacRae, but Jewel Mallory. She had to remember that.

Annie chattered all the way to the car. Tavia loved the lilt of her laughter, and she found herself almost excited to be going home with them. Though she'd never been much of an actress, had even failed drama class her sophomore year in high school, she was going to have to be on her toes every minute of every day. The last thing she wanted to happen was for them to find out in a way that would hurt them.

"I've told all our friends they have to wait until you're more fully recovered before they come to see you," Annie went on. "When you're feeling better, we want to have a big party for you. Invite all of them so they can meet the woman Adam chose to be his wife. Would you like that?"

Tavia nodded, but inwardly she wanted to shout out a big "No!" Being among their friends and having to answer questions about her relationship with Adam would add more pressure that she cared to take.

The fancy car parked under the hospital's canopy took Tavia's breath away. She'd never ridden in such a fine car. It smelled like new leather. She noted Annie had filled the back seat with plump pillows and a blanket to make her ride more comfortable, which she greatly appreciated. Though her ribs were paining her, once she settled in and Annie propped the pillows around her, she was actually fairly comfortable.

The drive to the Flint home up in an area near Eldorado Canyon was beautiful, and farther than Tavia had expected. Dr. Flint turned the car onto a road leading off the highway into the Denver foothills, and toward the little town of Eldorado, eventually coming out onto a plateau-like area. It was a gorgeous day. The air was clean and fresh, without a cloud in the sky.

James smiled at her in the rearview mirror, causing Tavia to remember how Adam had smiled at her in that same way. She hadn't realized how much the two men looked alike until she caught the glimpse of James's eyes framed in the mirror. "You picked a good day to come home. It was a bit cloudy yesterday and much cooler."

Tavia smiled back at him. "Nice—day."

Annie turned in her seat to face her, much as Jewel had done just minutes before the accident. "I'm glad you're here with us."

Without taking his eyes off the road, James cupped his wife's shoulder. "Now, Annie. Don't rush our little girl. You two will have plenty of time for visiting. If I have my way, Jewel will be with us for a long time."

Annie muffled a snicker as she reached to pat her husband's hand. "You may never get away from this man, Jewel. He's as excited about having you with us as I am."

Tavia's breath caught as James maneuvered the car through an iron gate and up a short, tree-lined driveway to an elegant, sprawling Spanish-style home. This was where the Flints lived? This was to be her home while she recuperated?

"Well, here we are. Home. *Mi casa es su casa.*"

She remembered reading those words painted in bright colors on the wall of a Mexican restaurant where she'd once worked. My house is your house.

James pulled the car as close to the front door as possible, then hurried out the driver's side to assist first his wife, then Tavia.

She wanted to scream out as she leaned to get out of the car. The pain in her ribs was nearly unbearable, but she bit her tongue and kept her silence, offering only a meek, "Thank you."

Both James and Annie helped her into the house, into a room more beautiful and inviting than any she'd seen in magazines. The walls were all stucco and painted off-white. The fireplace was lit, transmitting a warm, welcoming glow to the entire room. The furniture was a deep-burgundy leather, and covered with an abundance of throw pillows woven in combinations of every earth tone you could imagine. The floors were done in varying shades of beige and brown tile, and made a perfect backdrop for the many hand-woven area rugs scattered about the living room and hallway.

"I know you're tired from your trip home, Jewel." Annie nodded her head toward a long hallway. "We can show you the rest of the house later. Why don't I take you to Adam's room, where you can get some rest, maybe even a nap, and I'll bring you a nice cup of hot tea. Would you like that?"

Exhausted from both the trip and the mental strain of portraying herself as someone she wasn't, Tavia nodded. *I can't whisper forever. I have to talk to these people or they're going to know something is wrong.* She took a deep breath and let it out slowly, her hand going to her throat. "That—that would be—very nice. Thank—you."

Annie grabbed on to her hand. "Oh, sweetie. You don't have to try to answer if it hurts your throat. Just keep whispering. Hopefully, a nice cup of tea with two or three spoonfuls of honey will help soothe that throat of yours."

Taking her elbow, Annie led Tavia down the hall to a room at the far end. "This was Adam's room. We moved into the house when he was still in high school. Typical teenager, he wanted the one at the end of the hall so he could be off by himself so his loud music wouldn't disturb us." Annie paused, her hand caressing the smooth oak door. "The only thing we changed when he went off to college was to take down some of the posters he'd hung on the walls. Adam had a passion for Christian music artists. These walls were covered with their pictures."

Tavia braced herself in the doorway, peering cautiously into the room. She had to smile. It was the ideal man's bedroom. Heavy furniture. Big-screen TV. Tape decks. Speakers mounted in the wall. A desktop computer on the massive desk. Indirect lighting, as well as several large lamps on the chests and nightstands. But one thing seemed out of place in the room. The queen-size bed was covered with a lovely basket quilt, done in shades of blue, yellow, lavender and green, and it was hand-quilted with tiny, even stitches. And there, leaning against the pillows, Annie had placed the plush yellow bear Beck had bought for her. Tavia felt like running to it, grabbing it up and hugging it to her bosom. It had become her security blanket.

"Adam's grandmother made the quilt. She finished it a few weeks before she passed away. The next one was to be for Adam's eighteenth birthday. He'd picked out the colors and the fabric to match his room, but she didn't last long enough to finish it." Annie sat down on the bed and lovingly traced a finger across the tiny stitches. "He loved his grandmother. When she died, Adam asked for this quilt. Though it's not the masculine style he would have preferred, it was special to him because she made it."

"Your mother?" Tavia asked, amazed by the importance both Annie and Adam put on the lovely handmade quilt.

Annie's face took on a look of nostalgia. "Yes, my mother. I inherited my weak heart from her."

"I'm sorry."

"So am I. She was a wonderful mother." Annie stood quickly and busied herself taking the pillows off the bed and turning back the quilt. "Let's get that coat off you." She helped Tavia remove her coat, motioned her to sit on the bed, then pulled the house slippers and socks from her feet. "Be careful now. Don't hurt those ribs!"

Annie's concern touched her deeply. Once she was in the bed and Annie had covered her with the sheet and quilt, she leaned back into the pillows and tried to relax.

"You stay right there and I'll bring you that cup of hot tea. Will green tea be all right? It's supposed to help with healing."

Tavia nodded. "Green tea is fine. Thank you." Her words were coming a little easier now. Maybe, by tomorrow, the rawness in her throat would be nearly gone.

"Is it all right if I come in?"

Tavia lifted her head and smiled at James. "Of course."

He crossed the room and placed the bag Annie had brought from the hospital on a chest. "Anything I can get for you?"

Continuing to smile, she shook her head.

"Annie insisted you'd want to stay in Adam's room. I wasn't so sure that was a good idea. If you're uncomfortable staying here, we can move you to the guest room next door."

"It's fine. I like it."

James seated himself on the edge of the bed and sat gazing at her, his eyes filled with tenderness. "I guess Annie told you about the quilt."

Tavia nodded.

"Adam and his grandmother were very close. About as close as me and my dad. She was close to Annie, too. Did Annie tell you her mother had heart problems?"

"Yes."

He lowered his head and flattened a palm on the colorful quilt, spreading out his fingers. "It scares me to think how much Annie's health parallels her mother's."

Oh, James. You're making this even harder.

"Oh, good. James brought your bag in. I'll put it on the counter in the bathroom." Annie carefully crossed the room, a cup of steaming, hot tea in one hand and a glass of water in the other. "Dr. Stevens said it was all right if you took a pain pill. Do you need one, Jewel?"

Tavia shook her head. As long as she stayed perfectly still, the pain was tolerable. "No—thank you."

"Well, I'll put one here by your water glass, in case you need it later. I know it's hard for you to sit up with those ribs bothering you, so I brought a straw for your tea." Annie placed the water on the nightstand and knelt beside the bed, holding the teacup and offering the straw.

Tavia took a careful sip. The hot tea did feel good to her throat and the honey added just the right amount of sweetness. "Thank you, Annie."

Annie patted her arm. "You're welcome. I love you, and I'm so happy you're here with us."

Tavia reveled in those three words. Other than Annie and James, no one had ever told her they loved her before. Oh, Annie, I love you, too. More than you'll ever know. Living here with you like this is like living a fairy tale. If I could have my way, I'd live here forever.

"We're going to leave you alone." Annie rose and reached out her hand to her husband. "Try to rest. The nurse told me you didn't sleep well last night."

Tavia watched as the considerate couple left the room, then snuggled down beneath the quilt, ready to take a nap. She'd made her decision and, right or wrong, she would live with it. There was no turning back.

When she awakened, a tray was sitting on her bedside table, complete with a carafe of coffee, orange juice, a small dish of applesauce and a carton of strawberry yogurt. How thoughtful. Annie must have placed them there while she was sleeping.

Gritting her teeth against the pain, she worked her way out from under the quilt and slipped into the robe Annie had bought her, then slid her feet into the slippers. Going into the spacious bathroom, she splashed her face with water and finger-combed her hair, then added a slight dab of lipstick to her sore, cracked lips. Gazing into the mirror she took stock of her appearance. Her pale, tired face stared back at her and seemed to be saying, "You're not Jewel Mallory. How dare you try to take her place?"

She turned away, trying to block the image from her mind. Being careful not to jar her body and agitate her ribs, she moved across the thick carpet to the bed and poured herself a cup of hot coffee. She was about to take her first sip when a timid knock sounded on her door and Annie's smiling face appeared.

"I'll fix you some soft-boiled eggs, if you like."

Tavia pointed to the tray and answered in a soft whisper. "No, thank you. This is more than I can eat."

"Do you mind if I stay? I have some things I'd like to show you." Annie closed the door and moved quickly to the tall chest of drawers. "Adam cleaned out this chest when he came home for Christmas." She pulled one of the drawers open and lifted out a stack of sweaters. "I bought these for you. I hope they're colors you like. And I got these to go with them." She opened another drawer displaying pairs of both blue and black jeans. "I figured you and I were about the same size. There are a couple of pairs of sweat pants in here, too. I thought they might be easier to get on and off, with your arm in that cast."

Stunned by her thoughtfulness and generosity, Tavia sat speechless, staring at the lovely items.

"You'll find several new T-shirts in the third drawer, along with some underwear and socks, also white tennis shoes. I hope these will work for you until you feel like going shopping. What else do you need?"

Tavia sat in a daze. She'd never owned this much clothing in her life, and certainly not expensive clothes like these. "I can't—take all these—things."

Annie gave her a puzzled frown. "Of course you can. Adam wanted you to be a part of our family. I loved getting these things for you."

"Too—much."

"Too much?" Annie gave Tavia a teasing smile. "I thought young women never had enough clothes. I know that's the way I was when I was your age." Her face took on a melancholy look. "It gives us joy to do things for you, Jewel. Don't deprive us of that pleasure. Doing things for you is like doing things for Adam. James and I both need that. It's therapy for us."

Tavia didn't have a response. What could she say?

"James and I are going to run to the grocery store and pick up some things from the cleaners. He never gets the right things, even if I give him a list. Will you be all right here by yourself?"

Tavia nodded.

"Why don't you stay in bed and rest until we get back. The housekeeper is off today, so I put a kettle of soup on to simmer. We'll have an early lunch and, when you're up to it, we'll show you the rest of the house."

HOW TO GET YOUR
2 FREE BOOKS AND FREE GIFT

1. Peel off the 2 FREE BOOKS sticker from the front cover. Place it in the space provided at right. This automatically entitles you to receive two free books and an exciting surprise gift.

2. Send back this card and you'll get 2 Love Inspired® books. These books have a combined cover price of $9.98 in the U.S. and $11.98 in Canada, but they are yours to keep absolutely FREE!

3. There's <u>no</u> catch. You're under <u>no</u> obligation to buy anything. We charge nothing – ZERO – for your first shipment. And you don't have to make any minimum number of purchases – not even one!

4. We call this line Love Inspired because each month you'll receive books that are filled with joy, faith and traditional values. The stories will lift your spirits and gladden your heart! You'll like the convenience of getting them delivered to your home well before they are in stores. And you'll love our discount prices, too!

5. We hope that after receiving your free books you'll want to remain a subscriber. But the choice is yours – to continue or cancel, anytime at all! So why not take us up on our invitation, with no risk of any kind. You'll be glad you did!

6. And remember…we'll send you a surprise gift ABSOLUTELY FREE just for giving Love Inspired novels a try!

Steeple Hill®

SPECIAL FREE GIFT!!

We'll send you a fabulous surprise gift, absolutely FREE, simply for accepting our no-risk offer!

® and TM are trademarks owned and used by the trademark owner and/or its licensee.

Order online at: www.LoveInspiredBooks.com

©1997 STEEPLE HILL BOOKS

Books FREE!

DETACH AND MAIL CARD TODAY!

HURRY!
Return this card promptly to get
2 FREE books
and a FREE gift!

Love Inspired

YES, please send me the
2 FREE *Love Inspired* books
and FREE gift for which I
qualify. I understand that I am
under no obligation to
purchase anything further, as
explained on the opposite page.

affix
free
books
sticker
here

313 IDL D372   113 IDL D373

FIRST NAME

LAST NAME

ADDRESS

APT.#	CITY

STATE/PROV.	ZIP/POSTAL CODE

(LI-LA-05)

"I'll be fine," Tavia whispered. "Don't—don't worry about me."

"If I were you, I wouldn't bother about dressing today. You're still much too weak. Just stay in your gown and robe, okay?" Annie kissed her cheek again, then made her way out the door.

Tavia lay back against the pillow and pulled the quilt up over her. The late-morning sun was filtering into the windows through the stately pines surrounding the house, making lacy patterns dance on the wall. The last thing Tavia remembered before drifting off to sleep was the sound of James's car pulling out of the driveway.

When she awoke nearly two hours later, according to the clock on the night table, she was immediately treated to a wonderful aroma.

"Oh, good, you're awake. I was just coming to check on you. You've got company."

Tavia narrowed her eyes and stared at Annie, her heart racing. "Company?" Who would be coming to see her? Only Beck and Dr. Stevens knew she was here, and Dr. Stevens certainly wouldn't be making a house call. It had to be Beck.

Chapter Nine

Beck rose from his place on the sofa. "Hello, Jewel."

"Oh, Beck! It's you." Tavia smiled. "It's good to see you."

James stepped toward him and rested a hand on his shoulder. "Beck phoned right after we got home and I invited him over. He was concerned about you. I was just telling him it's still difficult for you to speak with the soreness in your throat from that tube, but you're managing quite nicely."

Annie helped Tavia to the sofa and plumped up a pillow to brace against her sore ribs. "Our girl has had a good nap, and I was just about to get her a nice hot bowl of cream of potato soup. We'd love to have you join us, Beck."

Beck shook his head and held a palm up between them. "No, ma'am, I couldn't. I don't want to impose."

"Impose? You're not imposing, Beck. This is the

housekeeper's day off so Annie fixed a big pot of soup. There's plenty for everyone," James chortled. "You don't know my wife very well. She doesn't take no for an answer. You might as well plan on staying. She'll never let you out the door without feeding you."

"James is right, Beck," Annie told him with a winsome smile. "I'm not about to let you go away hungry. It won't be anything fancy. We're only having soup. Dr. Stevens said to keep our Jewel on soft foods for a few days."

"Don't let Annie fool you with that not-anything-fancy line, Beck," James added with a wink toward his wife. "Her homemade potato soup is one of my very favorites."

Beck grinned his silly, bashful grin, the one that made Tavia want to laugh. There was something special about the man. He was different from any of the men she'd ever met. But considering the few chances she'd had to meet nice regular-type men, anything further with Beck would never happen. Not with the rut her life had been in.

Beck rubbed his hands together expectantly. "You've talked me into it, sir. Nothing warms your innards like a hot bowl of soup."

"Then it's settled. Give me five minutes in the kitchen to set the table and we'll have lunch."

"I—I could help." Tavia started to rise, but Annie hurriedly put a hand on her shoulder to stop her.

"You stay right where you are. We brought you here to nurse you back to health, and that's exactly what we're going to do."

Everyone turned as the front door opened.

"Hey, is that potato soup I smell?"

James shook his head with a grin. "Dad, we never know where you are, the way you come and go all day long, but let us put food on the table and, somehow, you find your way home."

"Which of your ladies were you with this morning, Grandpa?" Annie asked, her eyes sparkling as she headed for the kitchen. "Three of them have already called today asking for you. I left their names and numbers by the phone."

James turned to Tavia. "You'll get used to the phone ringing. My dad is quite popular with the ladies."

George Flint ran a hand through his healthy head of silver hair. "Can I help it if I'm handsome, gregarious, charming and a romantic at heart?"

James rolled his eyes. "No conceit in this family. My dad got it all!"

Grandpa leaned over the back of the sofa and kissed Tavia's cheek. "Don't you listen to him, Jewel. That son of mine has a tendency to exaggerate."

"Me, exaggerate?" James threw his arms open wide. "I've heard you tell some pretty tall tales."

The old man put a finger to his lips. "Quiet, now. You're going to give these nice people the wrong impression about me. Oh, by the way," he added with a glint in his eyes, "don't count on me for supper tonight. Two of the ladies from the Senior Center are fixing me homemade chicken and noodles. Homemade biscuits, too."

James hitched a thumb toward his father. "See what I mean? This man needs an appointment secretary."

Annie came back into the room, laughing and shaking her head. "He already has an appointment secretary. Me!"

James reached out to everyone as they gathered around the table. "Okay, gang, let's hold hands and thank God for our food and for finally allowing our precious Jewel to be home with us where she belongs."

His prayer pierced both Tavia's heart and her conscience.

George gave her hand a squeeze. "He's right. We're all glad you're home."

Annie nodded. "And what she needs right now is some hot soup to soothe that sore throat of hers."

Though Tavia had to take small spoonfuls of the hot soup, it felt good to her throat and, much to her surprise and the surprise of the others at the table, she consumed the entire bowlful.

After their pleasant lunch, James helped Annie clean up the kitchen while George took a phone call from one of his many admirers and Beck and Tavia visited in the family room.

"It's sure nice to see you feeling better, Jewel." Beck sat opposite her in a chair near the fireplace. "We were all worried about you. Especially Annie."

She motioned toward her throat. "I'm getting better every day."

He leaned forward in the chair, resting his elbows on his knees. "Can I get you another pillow? Would you like the ottoman under your feet?"

She shook her head. Everyone was being so nice to her and she loved being in the Flints' home, but each time someone called her Jewel, she cringed.

"Are your ribs feeling any better?"

Stirred out of her thoughts by Beck's voice, she gave him a blank stare. "Ah, what?"

Beck took her hands in his, a worried expression on his face. "Are you okay?"

"I'm—all right. Honest. Just tired of lying on my back all day." Having his hands folded over hers felt so good. It was as though she could absorb his strength by being near him.

"Well, the kitchen is all cleaned up," James said as he and Annie came bustling back into the room. "Grandpa said to tell you both goodbye. One of his girl-friends called and wanted him to come and help her pro-gram the time into her VCR." He chuckled. "For a man of eighty-two, he sure gets around."

Tavia gasped. "He's eighty-two?" She would never have guessed George to be that old.

"Yes, and some of the women he dates are only in their early sixties!" Annie replied.

Beck rose and extended his hand to James. "I'd better be going. I don't want to tire Jewel, and I have an appointment with the physical therapist."

James glanced down at the man's leg. "Looks like you're getting around pretty well now."

"Yes, sir, I am, but I have a long way to go before I can drive a truck again." He turned toward Annie and Tavia. "I've enjoyed having lunch with you. Thanks for inviting me."

Annie gave him a sweet smile. "It was our pleasure, Beck. You're welcome in our home anytime. We know you're concerned about Jewel."

He gave her a timid smile. "Yes, ma'am, I am concerned about her, and I'm concerned about you, too."

"I'll walk you to the door, Beck." James nodded toward the two women. "I think you two need to rest. Annie, as soon as you make sure Jewel is settled, why don't you try to take a nap?"

Annie smiled at her husband. "I may just do that."

Once Annie had tucked Tavia back under the quilt, kissed her cheek and told her how much she loved her, she sat down on the side of the bed. "We need to talk."

Tavia held her breath. What could Annie want to talk to her about?

"We've heard from the insurance company. They're ready to pay off the claim on the SUV. James and I discussed it, and we're wondering if you'd prefer something smaller. Maybe a Mercedes convertible like mine."

A Mercedes convertible? The only vehicle I've ever

really owned is that junker truck someone gave me, and it doesn't work anymore.

"I know it'll be a little while before you're ready to drive again, but you might be thinking about what kind of car you'd like to have. James said he'd stop at the car dealer's and pick up some brochures for you." Annie stood. "We want to make sure you get what you'd prefer. Oh, and the insurance agent said since Adam had made you his beneficiary, to call them when you're ready to settle the claim on—" she paused "—Adam's death."

"I'm—I'm not ready yet."

"That's what I told them. Try and get some rest. I'm going to lie down, too. I am a bit tired. From all the excitement of bringing you home, I guess."

Tavia tried to settle in, but couldn't get comfortable. Maybe, she reasoned, if they get me a car, I can load up what few things I have and simply drive away, leaving a note behind to explain everything. Then, once I'm back in Denver, or maybe Colorado Springs, I can abandon the car, take a bus or a taxi somewhere, and let the police find it.

It sounded like a good plan, but in her heart, she knew it would be difficult do it that way. The shock might kill Annie, devastate James and no telling what it would do to Beck.

The doorbell! Was Beck coming back again? She strained to listen but the voices coming from the foyer were too muffled to tell who it was. Relax. Maybe you're worrying needlessly. Maybe it's only one of Grandpa's many girlfriends.

But her complacency turned to trepidation as the door to her room was pushed open a crack.

"Jewel?" James spoke in a whisper.

"Yes, I'm awake."

"Do you feel like coming out into the living room? The sheriff wants to talk to you."

Beck left the therapist's office and hobbled to his rental car. He couldn't get those big blue eyes out of his mind. There was something about Jewel Mallory that made him want to pick her up and hug her. He'd felt that way since the first time he'd gone to her hospital room to visit her and sat by her bed waiting for her to regain consciousness. He'd heard of love at first sight, but surely it didn't happen. Especially not to him.

He climbed into the car, hooked his seat belt and put the key in the ignition. I feel sorry for her, that's all. I've got to put these crazy thoughts out of my mind. No wonder the doc wants me to have some counseling sessions. I must be going daffy. He started the engine and moved the car out onto the road. I'm stargazing about a woman who was about to be married.

Without thinking about it or planning it ahead of time, he pulled into the little strip-mall parking lot, right in front of the flower shop.

* * *

Sheriff MacGregor stood and yanked off his hat when Tavia entered the room. "Good afternoon, ma'am. I hope you're feeling better today."

"I am feeling much better, thank you." Was it her imagination or did the sheriff seem a little edgy? Tavia made her way to a large upholstered chair near the window and, with James's assistance, sat down.

"We discovered something at the accident scene. I'm hoping you can help me."

Tavia stared at the man, the beat of her heart booming in her ears so loudly it made it impossible to think.

Chapter Ten

James stepped in before the sheriff could go on. "Jewel has been through so much physically and she lost Adam, Sheriff MacGregor. Does this really have to be done now?"

"I'm afraid so, James."

James gave his head a shake. "Well, if you think it's necessary, I guess you have to do your duty."

Sheriff MacGregor reached into his pocket and pulled out a small plastic bag. "We found this at the scene of the accident." He opened the little bag and let something fall into the palm of his hand.

Tavia recognized it the second she saw it.

"It was a few yards from the guardrail, close to where you landed when you were thrown out."

"Well, then, it's probably hers," James said, frowning and seeming a little impatient.

"Maybe yes, maybe no." Sheriff MacGregor handed it to Tavia. "Tell me, ma'am, does this belong to you?"

She felt herself trembling. No doubt about it. The ankle bracelet was hers. The tiny little *T* engraved on it stood for Tavia. She'd bought it for herself at one of those discount houses, off a rack that had ankle bracelets each with a letter of the alphabet hanging on it, all priced at $4.95. But if she said it was hers and everyone thought she was Jewel, why would it have a *T* on it? No, she had to let them think she'd never seen it before. This was not the way to have the truth come out. Working to keep her emotions in check and her voice from wavering, she handed it back to him. "I've never seen it before."

"With that *T* on it, I didn't think it was yours, but I wanted to make sure. I thought perhaps it had belonged to someone special and you'd kept it for that reason. So I had to ask." He dropped the little bracelet back into the bag and stuffed it into his pocket. "I'll be going now. I don't want to take any more of your time."

Feeling somewhat relieved, Tavia leaned back into the sofa. "Thank you for bringing it by, Sheriff."

Trying to hold on to her emotions, she watched as James walked the sheriff to the door and said goodbye.

"That was strange." James rubbed at his chin. "Why didn't he just pick up the phone and call, instead of coming all the way out here to ask you about that bracelet?"

The old fear returned. Yes, why did he make a trip

all the way out here? Does he suspect I'm not who everyone thinks I am? Maybe I'm just being paranoid.

Beck stopped by after dinner with the flowers he'd bought at the florist shop. Miniature pink and white roses with springs of baby's breath in a white hobnail vase, and mounted on a stick tucked in between the blossoms was a tiny little china ballerina in a pink satin-and-net tutu.

"It made me think of you," Beck told her as he placed it on the coffee table in front of her.

Tavia's heart swelled with gratitude for his kind deed. "Oh, Beck, I love it!"

Annie bent and took in the sweet fragrance of the roses. "They're wonderful, Beck. How nice of you to bring them." One hand went to her forehead as she frowned. "I feel one of my dreadful headaches coming on. If you two don't mind, I think I'll go on to bed. James had a meeting in town, and Grandpa—" She rolled her eyes. "Who knows where Grandpa is. I can't keep track of that man."

Beck's eyes widened at her comment. "Surely at his age, he doesn't drive these mountains at night."

"Grandpa drive at night? No way! His girlfriends do the driving." She snickered. "Remember, we told you most of his girlfriends are in their sixties. I'm sure you'll be meeting them. He brings them by the house often."

Annie pointed toward the entertainment center. "Why don't the two of you watch a video or the TV."

Beck seemed surprised by her invitation. "Maybe I'd best be running along. That physical therapy session wore me out."

Tavia wished he wouldn't go. She loved being around him, but knew it would be improper to beg him to stay. "I'll walk him to the door, then stay by the fire for a while," she told Annie. "I'm really not sleepy. Not with that nap I had today."

"Just don't stay up too late. You've had a big day," Annie cautioned as she told them both good-night then headed for her room.

Beck reached out his hand and assisted Tavia to her feet. "I'm glad to know you're feeling better. I was really worried there for a while. You looked so helpless, lying in that hospital bed with your broken arm and that tube going down your throat. You have no idea how I prayed for you."

She stared down at their locked hands. "It—it seems everyone was praying for me."

"Which is probably why you're doing so well."

The subject of prayer was foreign to her and one of the last things she wanted to talk about. "Tell me more about yourself, Beck. We didn't cover much the other day."

Holding tightly to his cane, Beck let loose of her hand and cupped her elbow as they slowly walked to the door. "Not much to tell. I'm on the road most of the time so I don't do much but work and go to church."

"Don't you want to settle down someday? Get off the

road maybe?" Much to her surprise, she found she no longer needed to talk in a whisper. Her throat felt almost natural.

He appeared thoughtful. "Yeah, I'd like that, but only if I had a wife to share my life. Be pretty boring if it was just me rattling around in some house all alone. So far, God hasn't sent me the woman He'd have me marry."

She felt herself staring at him. "You really expect God will send you a wife? How would you know?"

"It's hard to explain. But I'd know. Maybe not at first, but as we got acquainted. I want His will for my life. Marrying the wrong woman would be disastrous."

And never meeting the right man can be disastrous, too. "You seem like the kind of man who'd want a houseful of kids. I'll bet you'd make a great dad." You're exactly the kind of man I'd like to marry, Beck. Kind. Considerate. Thoughtful.

Beck grinned. "Thanks. I'll take that as a compliment."

"I meant it as one."

"I think you'd make a great wife and mother. Adam was—" Beck pressed his eyelids together tightly. "I'm sorry. I'm not thinking straight. I'm sure it's still difficult for you to talk about him. I can only imagine how much you miss him."

I barely knew Adam! Oh, how I wish I could tell you that!

"I've heard so many nice things about your fiancé." He lowered his head and stared at the floor.

It was all Tavia could do to keep from reaching out and giving him a comforting hug.

"What's going on here?" James asked as he came into the family room through the garage door. "Beck, you look upset."

Beck bowed his head. "I'm so sorry, James. I can't sleep nights. I think about the accident every waking moment. Tell me what I can do to help make up for your loss? I have to do something before this thing drives me crazy!"

"You are working with a personal counselor, aren't you?"

Looking up at James with eyes filled with regret, Beck shook his head. "It's not helping."

James placed a hand on his shoulder. "Turn it over to God, Beck. Annie and I are trying to put our loss in God's hands. It's the only way."

Beck gestured toward Tavia. "But take a look at Jewel. That accident took her fiancé. How can I forget that?"

"You can't forget it. You never will, just as Annie and I will never forget the loss of our child. But, little by little, the hurt will go away. At least, that's what other Christians who have lost loved ones have told us. Only God can fill the void left in our lives and our hearts, but we have hope, Beck. We know Adam is in heaven with his Lord and, someday, we'll be reunited with him."

Beck ran the back of his hand across his eyes. "I know every word you're saying is true, but—"

"But you still feel responsible."

"Yes, sir. I do."

"You can't let this eat at you like a canker. You have a full life ahead of you. If you want to do something for Adam, live that life for God."

"I'll try, sir, but I have to do something, anything to make this up to you." Beck swallowed hard. "I'm a pretty good carpenter. It's always been kind of a hobby with me. Are there any jobs I can do around here? Build some shelves, add a closet, maybe construct a patio or a gazebo for you and Annie? I may have a bum leg right now, but my hands and arms are good and strong."

James gave him a placating smile. "I'll talk to Annie and see if she's interested in a gazebo."

As Tavia watched and listened to their conversation, she was overwhelmed with Beck's gentleness and kindness.

"I'm glad you're still up," James told her after he'd said goodbye to Beck. "I knew you'd be needing some things so I went to the bank today and opened up a checking account in your name. You'll need it until you can get on your feet. Oh, and I added your name to our MasterCard account. When you feel up to it, I'll help you get your checkbook and credit cards replaced. Since you weren't able to give us information about your insurance coverage, I went ahead and assumed your hospital bill. I'm sure, under the circumstances, they'll reimburse me." He handed her an envelope.

"What's this?"

"Just a bit of cash. You can pay me back later."

Stunned by his words, Tavia stared at him. "You—you didn't need to do that, James. Annie has already bought me everything I need."

He lowered himself onto the sofa along with her and folded her hand in his. "If Adam had lived, he would have provided for you. That's what we Flint men do. We take care of the women in our lives. I'm taking care of you in Adam's place. Nothing would please Annie and me more than to have you stay here with us as long as we can keep you. Our home is your home. I want you to use that checking account and the credit card as freely as you would have if they had been established for you by our son."

"But, I've always worked and—"

"There's no need for you even to think about going back to work yet. As long as you need it, I'm going to provide for you. Don't say another word. It's already been decided and there is nothing you can do about it." He snapped his fingers. "Oh, yes. One other thing. I'm sure Annie talked to you about a car. I spotted a pale-blue Mercedes convertible at the dealership when I took my car in to have some work done on it. Since Annie thought it would be the perfect car for you, I went ahead and signed the papers and asked the dealer to deliver it in a day or two. If you don't like it, we'll trade it for something else."

Tavia couldn't help it. She began to cry. "You and Annie—you are so good to me. I don't deserve it. I—I—"

"Jewel, if for any reason you walked out of our lives tomorrow, I'm not sure Annie would survive. She is so happy to have you here with us. Because of you, Annie has made it through our loss of Adam. Please, for my sake, stay with us."

Tavia felt her heart sink. How could she ever tell them the truth with James talking like that? Did keeping Annie alive justify the lie she was living? Maybe she should just tell James the whole story and let him decide what to do. After all, he knew Annie and her condition better than anyone else.

They heard the front door open and close, then voices coming from the hallway.

"We're in here, Dad," James called out with a wink toward Tavia. "More of his girlfriends."

Within seconds, Grandpa appeared with two attractive older women. "Ladies, I want you to meet my son, James, and my new granddaughter, Jewel."

James gave them each a nod. "Nice to meet you, ladies."

The two women responded with smiling nods as they continued to hold on to Grandpa's arms.

"I promised us all a cup of hot cocoa before they drove on home." Grandpa nodded toward the kitchen. "Either of you want a cup?"

Both Tavia and James shook their heads.

"Let me know if you change your mind." Grandpa herded his guests past them and into the kitchen.

James reached out his hand and pulled Tavia to her feet. "Get used to it. That man has more lady friends than any man I know."

"I guess I missed their names," Tavia said, surprised Grandpa hadn't introduced them.

James harrumphed. "He probably didn't remember their names!"

As Tavia lay in bed, the day's events rotated through her mind, but two things stood out. The sweet, gentle spirit of Beck Brewster and the generosity of the Flints. While it would be nice to have a new car and money in the bank that was all hers, the thing she wanted more than anything else was to be able to stay with the Flints and be the daughter they thought she was. She'd never met such loving people. How easy it would be to stay and pretend she was Jewel. But realization struck and she knew that someday Jewel's body would be discovered and her make-believe kingdom would come tumbling down. She might even end up in prison. Was all of that worth the risk? Maybe she should take just enough money to get by until she was able to work again, and leave. Just disappear.

But as she went into her bathroom to prepare for bed, one look in the mirror at the ugly gash on her head and the cast on her arm, not to mention the pain in her ribs, convinced her she had no choice but to stay. At least, for a little while.

"Beck called to see how you were and I invited him for dinner," Annie told her when she came into Tavia's room the next morning.

Tavia was glad to see a smile on Annie's face. A good night's sleep appeared to have done wonders for her.

After a lazy breakfast and a simple lunch, both prepared by Celeste, the Flints' housekeeper, Annie gave Tavia a tour of the rest of the house. She'd had no idea it was so large. Each room was more splendid than the one before it, all done in Annie's favorite colors.

"And this," Annie said, pushing open a door off the hallway leading to the garage, "is the laundry room." She pointed to a white plastic sack resting on a shelf above the dryer. "Your bag of clothing is right there, but don't worry about it now. You can go through it when you're feeling stronger."

As Tavia stared at the bag her heartbeat quickened and her hands began to sweat. Was there anything in that bag that would lead to her true identity? "I'll take it in my room. No sense leaving it in here." She grabbed the bag and held it close.

Annie pulled the door closed. "Other than a storage room in the attic, I guess that's about it. You've seen the entire house."

James wandered into the hall and distracted Annie.

After taking advantage of the distraction, Tavia headed for her room, eager to check out the bag's contents.

Once there she quickly opened it. To her relief, although that ten dollar bill was still in her pocket, the key ring wasn't. But what if Annie had found it earlier and taken it out? No, she told herself, if Annie had found it, she would have told James and he would have called the sheriff.

Though her body was tired from being up so many hours, her brain wouldn't calm down and she found it nearly impossible to get to sleep. Eventually, she drifted off.

It was after five by the time she awakened, and Beck was due to arrive at six. With the pain still persisting in her chest and feeling stiff from lying in bed, she maneuvered herself into the bathroom to freshen up, then selected one of the sweaters Annie had bought for her, a pale-blue cable-knit one, and slipped it over her head. Struggling into a pair of brand-new blue jeans wasn't easy with her broken ribs, but she finally managed it. She finger-combed her hair, checked the mirror one more time, then made her way into the huge family room.

"There she is," Grandpa said, rising as she entered. Three ladies, all dressed in their finest, sat smiling on the sofa, lined up like Twinkies in a box. "Ladies, this is Jewel, my new granddaughter. Isn't she pretty?"

The three ladies, none of whom she had met before, nodded. Tavia had to smile. Though each had to be in their mid-to-late sixties, they were behaving like school-girls with a crush on the star quarterback as they gazed at Grandpa with adoring eyes.

"Let me introduce my friends. Dorothy, Kathryn and Helen." Grandpa paused, scratched his head and made a face. "Or is it, Kathryn, Helen and Dorothy?"

Tavia gave each a smile, then allowed Grandpa to help her into a chair.

"Where are you four going tonight, Grandpa?" Annie asked, an amused grin playing at her lips.

Grandpa wiggled his bushy eyebrows. "They're taking me to dinner at a new Mexican restaurant in Denver." He pulled one arm free long enough to give his watch a quick glance. "Then we're gonna catch a movie. Maybe go for ice cream afterward." Turning to James, he added, "Don't wait up for me, son. Might be pretty late. Way past your bedtime."

The three women giggled as James rolled his eyes. "Whatever you say, Dad."

Grandpa joined his guests on the sofa after pulling a photo album from a shelf and began showing them pictures of himself when he was in high school. He had such a cute way about him, and more energy than men half his age. *No wonder these women like being with him,* Tavia thought as she watched.

Beck arrived right at six. After a pleasant exchange of introductions and conversation, Grandpa and his doting entourage headed out the door and those remaining moved into the dining room. Once they were seated, James turned to Beck. "You want to ask God's blessing on our meal?"

Beck nodded and bowed his head. *"Father God, we come before You, humbled that You are concerned about every little thing in our lives. God, You brought the four of us together in a way none of us would have preferred, but who are we to question Your sovereign will."*

He paused, and Tavia, who was peeking through her lashes, wondered if he'd be able to go on.

Beck softly cleared his throat. *"We love You, Lord, and—"* He swallowed hard. *"Bless this food to our bodies, we pray. Amen."*

James put a hand on his shoulder. "It's okay, Beck. God knows the needs of our heart, even if we can't put them into words."

Celeste served a wonderful dinner of pot roast, mashed potatoes and gravy and all the trimmings.

"The roast is so tender," Tavia said, forking up a small bite. "It's delicious."

Annie beamed. "Anything Celeste prepares is good, but her pot roast is my favorite. I was hoping you'd like it."

When they finished, James rose and pushed his chair against the table. "Why don't we have our dessert and coffee in the family room?"

All agreed and James helped Annie from her chair while Beck assisted Tavia.

The cheesecake topped with strawberries was a real treat for Tavia. She ate every bite.

"It's so nice to have you here, Beck," Annie told him as she placed her napkin on the coffee table and leaned back in her chair.

Beck smiled, and Tavia's heart flip-flopped.

"Nice to be invited. I'm glad to see Jewel is feeling better, and it's good to hear her voice."

"I've talked it over with Annie," James said, turning toward Beck once Celeste had cleared away their dishes. "We both have projects we'd like to see done around here. I need a wall of shelves built in my study so I can put all of my reference books in one place, and Annie—"

"I want you to build a gazebo!" Annie interjected with enthusiasm, breaking into her husband's sentence.

"So," James went on, "we do have some projects for you to do around here, but only if we pay you for your time."

Beck shook his head. "No, sir, there'll be no paying me. I want to do this for you. You have to let me." He lowered his head. "I—I need to do it—for me, too. It's the least I can do."

James rose, smiling broadly. "Okay, we'll work that part out later. Let me show you what I have in mind for my study."

The two men wandered off down the hall, talking on the way about the materials that might be needed.

Annie leaned toward Tavia. "Are you cool? Do you need an afghan over you?"

She shook her head as she stared into the flickering flames of the fireplace. "No, thank you, I'm fine."

Twenty minutes later, the men returned. "Well, I don't know about the two of you, but I'm kinda bushed. I think I'll retire and read awhile before I go to sleep." James reached out his hand to his wife. "Annie? How about you? Want to join me?"

Annie took his hand and allowed him to pull her to her feet. "That sounds like an excellent idea."

Beck glanced at his watch. "I need to get along, too."

Annie placed her hand on her hip. "Now, Beck. You're staying at that cabin all alone and poor Jewel has been confined to a hospital bed, barely able to move. Why don't you stay and keep her company? I don't want her sitting here by herself just because us old fogies are tired out. You'll be doing us a favor if you stay."

He gave her one of his shy smiles. "Well, if you put it that way, I guess I could stay for a while. If Jewel doesn't mind."

"Please stay," Tavia told him, wincing as she answered to another woman's name. "I'd really like the company. My body is tired of having to lie flat in that hospital bed for so long. I really think being up and moving around is helping my ribs. They're still quite sore, but at least I can tolerate them better now that I don't have to stay in bed all the time."

Annie patted Beck on the shoulder. "Good. Then we'll leave you two alone."

Once they'd all said their good-nights and the Flints had retired, the two sorted through the videos, finding nothing they hadn't already seen or that either of them cared to watch.

"Nice night. Would you like to go sit on the patio for a while?" Tavia asked, gesturing toward the sliding glass doors.

"You feel up to it?"

She nodded. "If you'll get that afghan off the chair and help me wrap it about my shoulders."

He retrieved the afghan then helped her to her feet, slipping his hand beneath her elbow as they slowly walked out onto the patio.

"What a beautiful evening." Tavia pulled the afghan closer about her neck.

"Is it too cold for you?"

She loved the concern in his voice. "No, the night air feels good. I've been cooped up inside way too long."

He led her to one of the wrought-iron chairs along the railing and seated himself beside her. "The Flints are nice people. They sure have a lovely home."

"Yes, they are wonderful people. They're taking good care of me." She waved her hand toward the twinkling lights of cabins and houses nestled in the mountains. "Beautiful, isn't it?"

Leaning forward, he rested his elbows on his knees,

his hands clasped beneath his chin. "Sure is. Kinda makes you wonder about all the people who live there. What they do for a living."

"If they're happy," Tavia added.

"Life doesn't always go the way we plan. Mine sure hasn't."

She thought his voice sounded a bit melancholy.

"You and Adam were lucky to have found each other."

"You said you nearly married once."

He leaned back in the chair, locked his hands behind his head and stuck his long legs out in front of him, crossing his ankles and staring straight ahead. "Yeah, I nearly got married once," he finally said. "For a while there, I really thought God had led me to the woman I was supposed to spend my life with. I actually thought I loved her."

"What happened?" Tavia asked, concerned.

"We only dated a couple of months before we set a wedding date. I was on the road most weeks and only with her on weekends, but we really hit if off. She even attended church with me."

He uncrossed his ankles and leaned forward, a sadness blanketing his face. "The day before the wedding, I called her house and a young man answered. When I asked him who he was, he said he was her son. That pretty much ended things."

Tavia frowned. "Why would her son answering the phone be a problem?"

He let his shoulders rise and fall in a heavy shrug. "The day we met, she told me she'd never married and she certainly hadn't mentioned kids. Turns out she'd not only married, she'd been married twice, and had three children. She lied to me!"

Tavia flinched, his words going right to her gut.

"Maybe—maybe she had good reason for lying." She nervously moistened her lips.

"Is there ever a good reason for lying?"

Assailed by her scattered emotions, Tavia felt weak all over, breathless, as if he'd just punched her in the stomach and knocked out her wind.

"I don't want to marry any woman who still has a husband running around somewhere. To me, the marriage vows are sacred and should be honored above all costs. When, and if, I marry, it's gonna be for life—regardless of what happens." He gave her his shy grin.

"I'm sorry things didn't work out for you," Tavia said, for lack of anything else to say, an uneasiness plucking at her insides.

"I'm just thankful I didn't find out after we'd said our I do's. Been shying away from women ever since. Besides, with my work schedule, it isn't likely I'll meet me a fine woman with the same kind of standards I've set for myself. I'll never understand how folks can hurt one another like they do." His words were strangely solemn.

"I don't, either."

He reached across and covered her hand with his,

his brows lowering over his eyes. "How about your childhood? Was it a happy one? Were you a rich kid like Adam?"

She gave a laugh that sounded ridiculous even to her. "No, not a rich kid. In fact, at times—" She paused, wondering how much Adam had told the Flints about Jewel's upbringing. "I'd rather not talk about it. My life was like most any kid growing up." Another avoidance of the truth!

"What do you like?"

She sent him a quizzical look. "Like? What do you mean?"

"I was just thinking how little I know about you. Do you like country music? Classical? What?"

"Country, I guess."

"What's you favorite food?"

"Oh, I'd have to say big juicy hamburgers topped with cheese, pickles, onions and mayo."

Beck gave her hand a squeeze as his face lit up. "You're kidding, right? That's my favorite, too! With a little barbecue sauce."

"I could go for the barbecue sauce!" she added, smiling at him. "Now it's my turn. What's the best Christmas present you ever got?"

He paused for a thoughtful moment. "How about best two presents?"

"I'll accept two. What were they?"

"My first bike when I was six, and my first car. An

old junker my dad bought me, but it was mine, all mine. I loved that car. What was your best present?"

She lowered her head shyly. "I'm afraid you'll think I'm silly when I tell you. It wasn't much, compared to your gifts."

"I promise I won't. Tell me."

"Okay. It was a music box with a tiny little ballerina on top that danced when the music played. I kept my mother's picture in the lid. It hasn't worked in years."

"Do you remember the song it played?"

She nodded, swallowing hard at the lump in her throat. "'The Skater's Waltz.'" That music box had been the only reminder she had left of her mother. Now that her landlord had probably gotten rid of her few possessions, he'd probably put it in a Dumpster. "Do you like sports?" she asked, needing to change the subject.

"I love sports. Especially football. I don't get to go to many games, but I sure listen to a lot of them on the truck's radio when I'm out on a run. How about you?"

"I watch every game the Colorado Buffalos play on TV. I've always wanted to attend one of their games. I'm a real fan. I like basketball, too."

He reared back and gave her a big smile. "A woman after my own heart. What's your favorite flower?"

She gave him an impish grin. "I have two favorites. White daisies and pink roses."

He laughed. "Good answer. You really know how to make a guy feel special."

"You are special."

"I sure hope you think so. Here's another one. Do you like dogs?"

"I love dogs. Especially black labs. I've always wanted one."

His brows raised. "Black labs? Really? Those are my favorite, too. Looks like you and I have many of the same tastes."

"Looks that way." She rose and walked to the iron railing edging the patio and gazed at the sky. "Isn't it beautiful?" she asked dreamily, relishing this time spent with Beck. "I love looking at the stars."

Beck walked up beside her, grasping the railing with his hand. "God's handiwork is amazing, isn't it?"

Tavia let out a gasp. "Oh, look, there goes a shooting star! We get to make a wish!"

Beck turned and taking her hands in his, gazed into her eyes. "If you thought your wish would come true, what would you wish? What is the innermost desire of your heart?"

To be married to you, dear Beck. To spend my life at your side, doing everything I could to make you happy. "Ah, I'm not sure," she answered, hoping her face wasn't giving away the feelings of love and admiration inside her. "What would you wish?"

Tilting his head to one side, he pursed his lips. "What

would I wish for? Other than wishing God would undo the events of the past few weeks? I guess I'd have to say finding someone to share my life with me, but she'll have to be the right one. I'd rather remain single the rest of my life than be caught up in a bad marriage."

Oh, Beck, I'd like to be that right woman for you. Tavia shivered in the night air.

Beck noticed and hurried to the chair to retrieve the afghan where she'd left it. "Here," he said, spreading it over her shoulders then wrapping his arms about her. "We can't have you catching cold. Is that better?"

She snuggled into the warmth of his arms, enjoying the woodsy scent of his aftershave. "Much better."

"Do you want to go inside?"

She shook her head. "No, do you?"

He smiled down at her and tightened his grip. "It's nice out here. I—I like being with you."

"I like being with you, too." She turned her eyes heavenward again, but her mind wasn't on the stars or the moon. Her every thought was focused on the man standing so close to her she could feel his heart beating. Oh, Beck, if it could be like this always.

"Me and my brothers used to go on weekend camping trips with my dad sometimes. After everything would get quiet and I thought everyone was asleep, I used to sneak out of the tent and lie on my back by the bonfire and stare at the sky, wondering what it would be like to be an astronaut."

"I'll bet you had a great time, camping with your dad like that."

He nodded. "I did. I wouldn't trade those times for anything. Dad always managed to spend some time alone with each of us. We sure had some good talks. If I ever have kids, I'm going to be like my dad. He's always worked long, hard hours to provide for his family, and he'll never be a rich man, but he's my role model. That man was filled with love for us kids. For my mom, too. Now that us kids are grown and gone, those two are like newlyweds. I think their love has grown stronger each year. I'm going to love my wife like that." He let loose a little chuckle.

Tavia twisted slightly and gazed up into his handsome face. *That's the kind of love I want, Beck. I have so much love to give. If only I could give it to you.* "I—I hope you find her."

He smiled down at her. "If I'd met you before Adam did, I would have thought you were her." He stiffened and pulled his arms away, letting them fall awkwardly at his side. "I—I mean—there's so much about you. You're the kind of person, well, you have so many good traits." He gazed at her for a moment, the offered his hand. "Maybe I'd better get you inside before—" He paused. "Before it gets any cooler."

Tavia accepted his hand then stood on tiptoes and kissed his cheek. "You're quite a man, Beck Brewster. The woman who gets you as a husband is going to be a lucky woman."

He grabbed her, pulling her into his arms and kissing her before she knew what was happening. She knew she should pull away, maybe even slap him, but she couldn't, nor did she want to. Instead, she leaned into his embrace and fully participated.

When they finally separated, he backed off with a look of embarrassment. "Oh, Jewel, forgive me. I don't know what got into me. I had no right to do that. Please don't tell the Flints. They'd never forgive me."

She reached up and cupped his cheek with her hand. "Nothing to forgive. I was as much at fault as you were." Turning, she walked across the patio and into the house, her heart swelling with emotion.

"I enjoyed our—talk," he said awkwardly when they reached the front door.

"Me, too." *More than you can possibly imagine!*

He lifted his hand slowly, his palm finally gently settling on her cheek. "I'll stop by tomorrow afternoon to see how you're doing— If you're sure it's okay."

"I'd like that."

"Hey, young lady, looks like it's gonna be just the two of us," Grandpa said, rushing to help her as Tavia made her way into the family room the next morning. "James had to go to church early since he volunteered to teach a class, so Annie went along with him. I told them I'd stay here and keep you company."

"You didn't need to stay. I would have been fine by

myself." She carefully lowered herself onto the sofa, her ribs stiff and sore from lying in bed all night.

Celeste came into the room wearing a pleasant smile. "Mrs. Flint said to bring in your breakfast tray as soon as you woke up. I hope you're hungry. I made you a breakfast burrito."

"Hey, how about me?" Grandpa's face bore a teasing smile. "Didn't you bring one for me?"

Celeste put the tray down then turned to him, shaking her finger in his face. "You've already had three, but there's another one in the kitchen if you want it."

He grinned. "Put it in the refrigerator. I'll eat it later, but I would take another cup of coffee." He tugged on her apron string, untying it. "You make the best cup of coffee in the world, Celeste."

She rolled her eyes as she retied her apron. "You are such a flatterer. No wonder you have so many women friends!" With that, she spun around and made her way back into the kitchen.

"Seems you have all the women wrapped around your little finger."

Grandpa grinned at Tavia, his eyes sparkling with mischief. "I like women, I value them, and I know how they like to be treated, that's all. Had nearly sixty years of experience with James's mother. Now that was a good woman. God was good to me when he let me be married to that gal. She was a real looker, too. I always called her my honey-babe."

"Where do you meet all these women? The way James and Annie talk, you have dozens of them calling you every week."

Grandpa fingered his chin thoughtfully. "Mostly at the Senior Center, I guess. Some at church. Some at the mall where I walk occasionally for exercise. Some of them even invite me to their place for a home-cooked meal. I take them up on it, too. We have a great time together."

His manner made Tavia smile. "I think that's great."

"Great for me and great for them. Us older folks have as much right to have fun as you younger ones. I make it plain—right up front—I have no interest in marrying any of them. We're all just good friends, sharing our lives and interests with each other."

He filled their coffee cups from the insulated carafe. "Now, tell me about yourself. I know Adam said your parents died in an automobile accident when you were a senior in high school and they were all the family you had, but I've never heard how the two of you met."

Tavia was glad he'd asked a question to which she knew the answer, remembering how Adam had grinned proudly when he'd told her about his and Jewel's first meeting. Willing herself to be calm as she told her first big story as Jewel, she began. "Actually, we met at an ice-skating rink. I'd seen him before and really wanted to meet him, but didn't know how. So one evening, I skated past him and managed to fall down right in front of him. Being a gentleman, he picked me up and skated me over to the side and stayed with me until he was sure I was okay. Then he asked me to skate with him. After that evening, we spent every spare minute together."

"Sounds like my grandson was a chip off the old block."

Tavia gave him a smile. "I'm sure he was."

"So how long was it before he asked you to marry him?"

She searched her memory. *Did Adam tell me that? Let's see. He said something about six months. Oh, I can't remember.* "Probably six or eight months." She was relieved when he seemed to accept her answer.

Grandpa's face took on a melancholy expression. "My wife and I liked so many of the same things. Guess you and Adam were the same way."

"Most of the same things. Except for rhubarb. Adam hated it, but he told me his mother loved it almost as much as I do."

"Annie does love it. If she knows you like it, too, I'm sure she'll have Celeste bake one of her famous strawberry-rhubarb pies. I hate the stuff myself. So does James."

Tavia delivered a smile. "That sounds wonderful! Wish I had a piece right now."

"Maybe by next Sunday you'll feel like going to church with us."

Church? I haven't been to church since the time I went on Easter Sunday with one of our neighbor girls.

The old man pulled off his glasses and rubbed at his eyes with arthritic fingers before going on. "I praise God for you, Jewel. You're like an angel sent from heaven."

Chapter Eleven

Beck came nearly every day the next week, taking measurements and going through magazines with James, helping him decide on what type of shelving he'd like in his study. Annie always invited him to have either lunch or supper with them, sometimes both. Though he or Tavia never mentioned the kiss they'd shared on the patio, she loved sitting in the chair watching him, listening to his conversations with Annie and James. And Grandpa, too, when he was home and not out on one of his many dates. Though Beck still wore his walking cast, he was getting around with very little trouble, and his spirits seemed better, for which Tavia was grateful.

Several days, Beck brought fresh bouquets of flowers to her. Simple bouquets, ones he'd picked out himself. She imagined what it would be like to be married to a thoughtful, responsible man like Beck.

After lunch Friday afternoon, Annie suggested Tavia ride into town with Beck to pick up some brackets and other supplies he needed to finish the shelves. At first, she refused. She longed to spend more time with Beck, but being with him, knowing each day she was falling more and more in love with him, was sheer misery. She claimed she was a bit tired, but when Annie insisted, telling her it would be good for her to get out of the house, she finally agreed.

"You feel like coming into the lumberyard with me?" Beck asked as he pulled into a parking spot near the door. "I hate to leave you out here in the car by yourself."

"Of course, I feel like it. My ribs don't hurt nearly as much as they did, neither does my arm." She waited until he opened her door and helped her slide to the ground, then put her hand into the crook of his arm when he offered it. Her heart fluttered. Most of the men she'd known would have rushed on ahead of her, without even looking back to see if she was coming. Not Beck. He may not have dated many women, but he was a gentleman through and through, and being with him was a real joy.

"Hey, I haven't seen you two for several weeks now. How're you both getting along?"

Tavia recognized the voice immediately.

"Doin' okay, Sheriff." Beck reached out and shook the man's hand. "Thanks for asking."

The sheriff glanced toward Tavia. "How about you, Jewel?"

Would she ever get used to that name? "I'm getting along fine. Annie and James are taking good care of me."

"Sure glad to hear it." The sheriff pulled his hat off and scratched his head, all the time keeping his eyes focused on her. "I think about the two of you every time I pass that spot on the highway. Nasty accident."

She couldn't help but fidget. Why was he looking at her like that? Feeling on the verge of anxious tears, she lowered her head, avoiding the sheriff's beady eyes.

"Well, I'd best be getting along. Got to get to the office." He put his hat back on and tugged it low on his brow. "Give my regards to the Flints."

"Sure will." As soon as the man was out of sight, Beck leaned close to Tavia, taking her hand in his. "Are you okay? You seemed a little upset."

"I—ah— It's—it's still hard to talk about the accident."

Beck slipped his arms about her and tugged her to him, holding her tight and resting his head against hers. "I know. It's hard for me, too."

She gazed into his eyes. How she longed to kiss him. "Give me a minute and I'll be okay."

Sunday arrived and Tavia had no choice but to attend church with the Flints. She was relieved when she learned they'd invited Beck to attend, too. Though she felt uncomfortable and had no idea what the pastor was talking about in his message, she had to admit she enjoyed the music. But the best part was getting to sit between Beck and Annie. Several times while holding the hymn book, hers and Beck's hands touched. It was one of the nicest feelings Tavia had ever experienced.

By Tuesday, Beck had fastened the support boards onto the wall and was nearly ready to start adding the shelving. Tavia loved to watch him work. He was a masterful carpenter. Every little joint had to fit perfectly before he was satisfied. Sometimes, she stood by his side wearing his nail apron tied about her waist, handing him handfuls of nails as he needed them. He actually joked about making her his permanent assistant and the two of them going into the carpentry business together.

"You're a wonderful carpenter," James told him one evening as he ran his hand over a section of the finished shelving. "I'm surprised you didn't go into the business. I could probably set you up with four or five doctors I know who would love to have this quality of shelving in their offices."

"No, sir. Not me. I'll stick to truck driving. This is just a hobby."

"Well, if you change your mind, let me know. I've already bragged to several about the work you're doing here." James ran his fingers over the finely sanded shelving again. "By the way, how's the counseling coming? I'm thinking of maybe checking into it for Annie and me. We could both use it. Though we don't say much about it, neither of us is doing a very good job recovering from Adam's death." He turned to Tavia. "How about you, Jewel? It might be good for you, too."

"Might not be a bad idea, sir," Beck inserted before she had a chance to answer. "It's really helped me. Thanks to my sessions with the counselor, I'm beginning to accept the fact that the accident wasn't my fault, that I did everything I could to avoid it." He lowered his head and fiddled with the handle of his finish hammer. "But then I get back to the cabin and get to remembering. I'm not sure I'll ever get over it."

"Annie tries to put up a good front, but she cries herself to sleep every night. I went with her to her doctor's appointment yesterday. He was quite concerned about her. She's lost more weight, and she's really edgy. I told him about Jewel living with us now, and he said that was the best thing that could have happened to Annie. It gives her something to take her mind off Adam and a reason to go on living."

Tavia sucked in a deep breath, sure she was going to faint. Why did all the responsibility for Annie's condition always seem to rest on her shoulders? She hadn't actually told anyone she was Jewel. Everyone had just assumed it. Each day, her deception was growing harder to live with, but what choice did she have?

"You didn't answer, Jewel. Do you feel counseling sessions might help you?"

She stared up into James's face. The last thing she wanted was counseling. Lying to the Flints and Beck was difficult enough, a counselor would probably see right through her. "No, I don't think so. At least, not yet. Maybe later. A few weeks from now."

"Jewel, dear, some of Adam's old friends from high school are in town and they want to meet you," Annie said when she came into Tavia's room the next morning. "I've invited them for dinner."

"Adam's friends?" A surge of panic rushed through Tavia. How could she ever meet Adam's friends without them discovering she was a fraud?

Annie sat down on the bed beside her. "It'll be fun. It's about time we began to invite people into this house again. Thanks to having you here, I'm feeling a bit stronger. I haven't had a real bad spell with my heart since the night—" She blinked hard. "You know—"

"How many are coming?"

Annie's face lit up. "Five! Won't that be nice?" Her joyful mood suddenly turned somber. "I know it's going to be hard for you to talk about Adam, sweetie, but we have to go on with our lives. Adam would want us to."

The group of five young men arrived right on time. Though Tavia was dressed and ready to meet them, she hung back in her room until Annie came to get her. She was relieved when she found herself sitting between James and Grandpa at the dinner table.

After a pleasant dinner, everyone but Grandpa, who had made prior plans for the evening, all moved into the family room and began to tell stories about Adam and the crazy times they'd all had during their high school years. Two of the men had even gone to grade school with him.

"Was he as funny as he used to be in high school?" one of them finally asked Tavia when their conversation began to die down.

She nodded and donned a fake smile, hoping he wouldn't ask her to elaborate. "Oh, yes. He had a great sense of humor. He loved to laugh."

"It's still a bit hard for Jewel to talk about Adam," James said quickly, as if protecting her.

"But it's been fun listening to your stories," Tavia told them with a smile. "I'm sure he loved all of you."

By nine o'clock, Adam's friends had gone and the house was once again quiet. When Annie and James retired to their room, Tavia decided to sit in front of the fireplace in the family room and read for a while. She was about ready to turn out the lamp when Grandpa came through the front door.

"How'd the evening go with Adam's friends?"

She closed her book and placed it on the table. "Fine. They had a good time reminiscing. I think Annie and James enjoyed it, too. Have you been out with one of your girlfriends again?"

He gave her a impish smile. "Yep. This one is begging me to marry her."

"But you're not interested?"

He gestured around the room. "Why would I want to settle down with one woman when I can live here in this nice house and date a host of women?"

He sat down by her and eyed her for a long time before he spoke again. "Why don't you ever talk about Adam? I'd think a woman who'd lost the man she loved would want to talk about him. Maybe ask questions about the years he'd lived before she met him."

Tavia's heart did a nosedive. Why had he asked such a question? Did he suspect she'd never really known his grandson? "It—it's hard to talk about him. Losing him was—terrible."

"He was a wonderful boy." Grandpa smiled. "Full of mischief, but he never did anything to really hurt someone."

"Like when he ruined his mother's famous cherry chocolate brownies?"

Grandpa reared back with a look of surprise. "He told you about that?"

She nodded. It was one of the few times she hadn't lied about Adam.

"I'll never forget the look on Annie's face when she opened the doors to the dining room and saw those brownies." Grandpa smiled. "That's the closest I ever saw that boy come to getting a real whipping. His father was as upset with him as his mother."

He rose to his feet, pulling her up with him. "About your bedtime, isn't it?"

She stood on tiptoe and kissed his cheek. "See you in the morning."

Tavia had no sooner reached her room than Annie slipped in the door. "Don't mind Grandpa. He means well. I heard him asking you why you never talk about Adam." Annie slipped an arm about her and gave her a hug. "I understand, sweetie. It's hard for me to talk about him, too. We women take things differently than men do. A man faces up to his grief. We women hide it in our hearts." Pulling away after giving her a compassionate smile, Annie backed out the door. "Good night, Jewel."

Tavia cringed and her stomach immediately went into a knot as the door closed behind Annie. She hated it when Annie called her Jewel, but had seen the love in Annie's eyes. Love for her.

She picked up the yellow bear from his place on her bed and stared at his funny little face. *I love Annie and James. I love Beck, too, but I'll never be able to tell him how much I love him. How could my life have ever gotten in such a mess?*

Over the next couple of weeks, Beck finished up the shelving and began work on the gazebo, with plans to have it finished in time for the big party Annie and James were throwing to introduce Jewel to all their friends. Tavia continued to help him by taking measurements, handing him tools and power cords, one-handedly sanding joints and all sorts of things. His laughter and his humor made her heart sing. Never had she been so happy. Though he never mentioned the kiss, she could tell he enjoyed being with her, too. But she knew—even if he felt the same attraction she was feeling—he would never say anything about it, thinking it was much too early to be speaking about such things to a woman who had so recently lost her fiancé.

Even though Tavia did everything she could to discourage Adam's parents from throwing such a big party, they kept telling her how proud they were of her and how eager they were to have everyone meet her and get to know the lovely woman Adam had asked to be his wife.

The day the doctor permanently removed Tavia's cast, Annie insisted the two of them go into Denver to celebrate and to shop for dresses for the party. It was to be a fiesta theme, and according to Beck, the gazebo would be ready in plenty of time for decorating.

By a few minutes past noon, the two women were seated in one of Denver's fanciest restaurants. After Annie prayed, they enjoyed elegant chef salads and dainty bread sticks. Annie went on and on about her plans for the party, the party specialists she had hired to do the invitations, the decorating and the catering.

"It's going to be so much fun!" she said. "There'll be colored lights, streamers in bright reds, blues, greens and yellow, piñatas, a mariachi band and wonderful Spanish food. I know of this little place that specializes in Southwestern-type party dresses. We'll go there as soon as we finish our lunch. I've already ordered those fancy black velvet sombreros with all the beadwork for James and Grandpa and Beck."

Tavia smiled inwardly at the thought of handsome Beck Brewster in a sombrero.

"We're asking all the guests to come in Southwestern attire," Annie went on. "I'm even inviting some of Grandpa's girlfriends. That should add some excitement."

Tavia laughed. "Do you think that's a good idea? Won't they be jealous of one another?"

"I doubt it. They already compete for his attention. When I asked him about it, he said to invite all of them. They were used to sharing him with one another. Isn't that funny?"

As soon as they finished their meal and the dishes had been removed, Annie pulled a small velvet box from her purse and pushed it toward Tavia. "For you. To celebrate having your cast off."

"I can't take any more gifts from you, Annie. You've already done too much for me."

Annie placed the box in her hand. "Open it, please."

Tavia gasped as she lifted the lid.

"It's Adam's baby ring. I wanted you to have it. I placed it on a fine gold chain." Annie reached across and pulled the delicate chain from the box, rose and fastened it about Tavia's neck. "I know how much you loved my son and the joy you brought into his life."

Touched by Annie's generosity and such an unselfish act being bestowed upon her, Tavia could no longer hold back her tears as she fingered the tiny circle of gold. "I can't, Annie. I know how much this ring means to you. You keep it."

Annie patted Tavia's arm, her own eyes misting. "I want you to have it, Jewel. It's one more thing to bond the two of us together, a symbol of my love for you. Please say you'll keep it."

Tavia nodded, unable to speak as mixed emotions flooded through her. *I'll keep it but only until I feel the time is right to leave you. I could never walk away with something this precious.*

Once Annie had signed the bill, the two women hurried off to the store she'd told Tavia about. After trying on at least a dozen dresses, they settled on two of the most colorful ones, with loads of embroidery on them, and two heavily ruffled petticoats to wear under them.

"This has been a wonderful day," Annie told her, wrapping her arm about her when they reached home. "I've never had a daughter to take shopping, now I have you. God knew I needed you when He took Adam." She kissed Tavia on the cheek, gave her a wave and headed off toward the bedroom with their packages.

The next day, the dealer delivered Tavia's new car: the powder-blue Mercedes convertible. She nearly fainted when Annie handed her the keys and told her it was all hers. Tavia couldn't believe the comfort of the leather seats as she sat behind the wheel. It was pure luxury!

"I'm going into Denver to spend the day with a friend," Annie told her as they walked back into the house. "Why don't you take a walk and check out your new car? It'll do you good to get out of the house for a while."

Tavia waited until Annie had gone, then pulled on a pair of jeans and a sweatshirt and headed for her new car. Despite Annie's suggestion, she intended to take it to the site of the accident that had changed her life. Since she still didn't have her license on her, or insurance for that matter, she'd have to drive extra carefully.

It didn't take long to find the spot. She remembered one of the roadside signs she'd noticed just before Beck's truck had begun to overtake them. Fortunately, the traffic on the highway was fairly light. She flipped on her flashers, pulled off onto the shoulder, and got out of the car. After sucking in a deep breath, she walked to the section of the guardrail that had been replaced after the accident. Her heart racing, she stared over the edge and into the canyon below. She hadn't realized it was so deep. It was actually more like a gorge than a canyon, with a rapid stream rushing through it. Why hadn't they found Jewel? Had her body been thrown into that stream and washed on down the canyon? Cold chills ran through Tavia and her whole body shuddered, despite the warmth of the sun on her back. It could just as easily have been Jewel who was thrown out of the car as it went over the guardrail, instead of me. *Why, God, if you are real, didn't you spare that young woman's life and take me? She had so much to live for. I have nothing.*

But as she stared into the deep crevice, going over each thing that had happened since the accident, she realized *she* was the one who had survived. Not Jewel. Did that mean God *wanted* her to live? The Flints had welcomed her with open arms. They'd never even met their prospective daughter-in-law. They were happy having her living with them. They even said they loved her, and their actions proved it. Was it so wrong to let them believe this lie? Especially considering what the truth might do to them?

But her conscience spoke up, refuting every flimsy excuse she could come up with for carrying on with her deception. *You can't just step into someone else's shoes. What you're doing is a horrible thing. These are loving people who trust you. How can you do something like this to them? They deserve to know the truth, regardless of the outcome.*

Tavia lifted her face and hands and shouted heavenward. *"God, I don't know if You're there or if You're even listening to me, but You have to believe I didn't willfully deceive these good people. I am going to tell them the truth. Soon. I promise. I have to."* She lowered her gaze to the deepest part of the gorge and with tears of remorse running down her cheeks, whispered softly, "Jewel, the sheriff said no one could have survived that drop into the canyon, so I'm sure you died instantly. But that's no excuse for me taking over your life and masquerading as you. You deserve to be found and have a Christian burial. I—I took that away from you by not telling everyone who I was when they took that tube from my throat. Wherever you are, please forgive me. I know it's a lot to ask, but I have no way to repay you for what I have done. All I can do is try, in some way, to live a better life and be there for the people I meet. Maybe I can volunteer or something. In your memory, and for what I have done, I promise I'll be a better person and find some way."

With one final glance into the depths of the canyon, Tavia walked back to her car and climbed in, her head resting on her hands as they circled the steering wheel. *"God, I mean it. I promise You I'm going to tell the Flints the truth. Maybe even tonight."*

"You okay, lady?"

She turned quickly to see a Colorado highway trooper staring through the window at her, his hand resting on the door frame. "I'm fine, thank you," she stammered, worried he'd ask for her license.

He gave the inside of her car a quick glance, then moved back to his car. She'd been so caught up in her thoughts she hadn't even heard the patrol car pull to a stop.

Tavia skipped lunch. She didn't feel like eating anything. James was at his clinic and Grandpa was spending the day at the Senior Center, helping with some fair they were putting on. Annie had said she wouldn't be home until late, so, other than Celeste, who was busy doing the laundry, she was all alone. She wandered through the house, making a mental picture of each room, knowing she'd never be seeing it again. She moved slowly back into the family room to wait for the Flints to return home. Beck called, and as much as she wanted to tell him she was not who he thought she was, she decided it was best to wait and tell the Flints first.

James came home about six with the news that Annie had decided to spend the night in Denver with her friend and wouldn't be back until the next day. His news made Tavia feel sick all over. It had taken her all these weeks to get her courage up to tell them, and now this!

"Oh, I nearly forgot. I met Beck at the lumberyard today. He wanted me to choose the finish for the gazebo. I invited him to come and have dinner with us. He should be here anytime." The words were barely out of his mouth when the doorbell rang. Tavia hurried to let Beck in.

After feasting on Celeste's cheese enchiladas, the four gathered in the family room in front of the fireplace. Tavia gazed into the flames as the men began to talk about the gazebo and the finish James had selected. Eventually, their conversation drifted around to God, heaven, Adam and answered prayers.

"You had to have been an answer to Adam's prayers,

Jewel. He would never have married a woman who didn't share his faith," James told her as he stoked the fire.

What should she say? How should she respond to his statement?

Before she could come up with an answer, Grandpa spoke up. "I think all us Flint men did pretty well in the wife-selection process. We Flints sure know how to pick our women."

Though Tavia joined in their laughter, inwardly, she was a bundle of nerves. She'd done many things in her life that would have displeased God, but those things were insignificant in comparison to what she was doing now.

James sat down and leaned toward her. She could tell he had something on his mind.

"Did Adam or Annie ever tell you about—our daughter?"

Tavia blinked hard. Did he say *daughter,* or had she misunderstood him? "You had a daughter?"

James nodded, the expression on his face reflecting pain. "Yes. As a part of this family, I think you should know. When Adam was a teenager, despite her doctor's warning, Annie decided she wanted another baby. Both the doctor and I did everything we could to talk her out of it, but she was adamant about it. He told her the risk was too great, but Annie was willing to take the chance. Her mind was made up. Eight months later, the doctor told her she was pregnant. Other than the day Adam was born, I've never seen her so happy."

He pulled out his handkerchief and dabbed at his eyes before going on. "All went fine until about a month before her due date, when the baby's heartbeat became irregular. Annie was confined to her bed and things seemed better for a while, then the baby stopped moving. The doctor had us meet him at the hospital and they performed a C-section." He paused, blinking several times. "Our baby was stillborn. A beautiful baby girl. Annie went into a deep depression. At times, I didn't think she'd ever come out of it. She hasn't been the same since. Until the day Adam told us about you, Jewel. You can't imagine the joy you've brought into our lives just by being here. You've given my Annie back to me."

Grandpa turned quickly to Beck. "I'm sure Jewel already knows this, Beck, but that's the reason Adam decided to be an ob/gyn. He wanted to be able to take care of women during their pregnancies, and do all he could to make sure those babies were delivered whole and healthy."

"He sounds like a fine man," Beck said meekly. It was obvious hearing about Adam's goal in life was adding even more to his remorse. "I wish I could have known him."

James reached across and placed his hand on Beck's knee. "I wish he could have known you, too, Beck." Standing to his feet, he stretched first one arm and then the other. "I'm beat, and I've got some reading to do in that medical journal I received today. If you don't mind, I'm going to my room."

Grandpa stood, too. "You'll have to excuse me, too. I've got some phone calls to return."

James frowned. "Kind of late to be returning phone calls, isn't it? Won't most of your ladies already be in bed for the night?"

Grandpa responded with a sly wink. "Naw, they're all expecting me to call."

James shook his head as his father walked off. "Dad, you are impossible."

"That's not what the ladies say!"

Once the two men had left the room, Beck scooted over onto the sofa beside Tavia. "I know that conversation about Adam and the baby his folks lost was hard on you. Can I get you a drink of water?"

"No, thank you." He was right. That conversation had torn at the very pit of her stomach. If only she could have told everyone the truth while she was psyched up for it. Now, it would have to wait until tomorrow. She glanced up at him and found him staring at her, his deep blue eyes riveted on her. *Oh, Beck, I love you. If only things were different between us.*

She had to turn away. Love between the two of them was not to be. She could only imagine the hate he would feel for her when he learned the truth.

Though she had turned away from him, Beck warily slipped an arm about Tavia's shoulders, and when she didn't protest, he pulled her close and gazed into her clear blue eyes. How could he have fallen in love with a woman he barely knew, one who had so recently lost her fiancé? His thoughts went back to the woman he'd been engaged to, the one he'd thought he loved. Had he really loved her, or was it simply an infatuation? The feelings he'd had for that woman were nothing compared to the feelings he had for Jewel. She was in his thoughts every waking moment, and in his dreams, too.

He shook his head to clear it. *She's just lost her fiancé, and she's way out of my league. As Adam's beneficiary, she'll never have to worry about money. Besides, the Flints have vowed they'll take care of her. She doesn't need me in her life. A lowly truck driver who still owes a bundle on his rig? Get real, Beck. You may love her, but what makes you think she could ever love you? What have you got to offer this woman?*

"I'm so sorry you've had to go through all of this. I know it's been hard on you," he told her, trying to make her understand his concern. It broke his heart when she began to cry.

"It helps to talk to you," she whispered as she leaned into his embrace.

Beck's heart pounded against his chest and he was sure, with her nearness, she could feel it, too. His lips seemed to have a will of their own as they moved toward hers. "I wish I knew how to take the pain away," he murmured.

Chapter Twelve

At first Jewel drew away slightly, and he was sure she was going to slap him and tell him to get out and never come back. But that didn't happen. Instead, she moved closer to him, into their tender kiss. Beck knew he should end this, apologize, but he couldn't. This was what he'd wanted since that evening on the patio. Even then, he'd told himself that what he was feeling was only sympathy and compassion. But there was a bond between them. He could feel it. The kind of love he was feeling was what a man was meant to feel for the woman he'd like to spend his life with. He knew it. That kind of love couldn't be denied.

Tavia leaned into Beck, enjoying the feel of his lips on hers, his arms wrapped about her. This was what she'd dreamt about, and it was happening again.

He's kissing me! The thought struck her like a bolt of lightning on a clear day. What am I doing? I'm supposed to be grieving! What if someone walked in and found us this way? She pushed away quickly, her hand going to her mouth.

"I'm sorry! I don't know what got into me!" Beck stood awkwardly and backed toward the hall. "Please forgive me. I didn't mean for that to happen again."

Tavia's mind was racing. She followed Beck to the hall. What could she say? What should she do? "It wasn't just you—it was my fault, too."

Grabbing on to her hand, he shook his head. "No, it was my fault. I must be crazy! I know I have no right, but I haven't been able to get you out of my mind."

"You feel sorry for me, that's all."

"No, that's not it at all! I—I love you. I know I shouldn't be saying this to you. You've just lost your fiancé! Besides, a woman like you would never want to get hooked up with a truck driver. I was out of my mind to kiss you like that again. Jewel, I've made such a mess of things. Promise you won't tell them what I've done."

Beck loved her! She'd wanted to hear those words.

"Please. I'll try not to let this happen again."

"I—I didn't tell them the last time, and I won't tell them now." But Beck, I want it to happen again.

"I—I've got to get out of here." He let go of her hand and hurried out the front door without another word.

Tavia stood in the middle of the foyer, her fingers pressed to her lips. Good-night, man of my dreams.

After twisting the lock on the door, Tavia tiptoed to her room. She dressed for bed and was about to crawl beneath the covers when she noticed the Bible on the nightstand. She opened it, hoping to find the things James and Beck had been talking about, confessing your sins and asking God for forgiveness. But the Bible was so big and had so many pages, she had no idea where to look. Frustrated and still trembling from her experience with Beck, she closed it, returned it to its place, and turned out the light, hoping sleep would blot out the many things dashing through her troubled mind. Even with the lights out, Beck's words about God and heaven haunted her. God could never forgive her, even if she asked Him. Here she was, answering to another woman's name, keeping the truth from people who believed she was to have been their daughter-in-law, and she'd fallen in love with a man who would hate her when he learned who she really was and how she had been deceiving everyone. And Annie. What about Annie? In desperation, Tavia cried out to God for mercy and forgiveness, asking Him to show her how to become a Christian.

When Annie returned home the next day, she was filled with excitement about the party and would barely let Tavia get a word in edgewise. With the party only two days away, rather than ruin things for Annie, Tavia decided to wait until it was over before telling everyone the truth. The invitations had gone out, the party planners had completed their work, and everything was in readiness. To tell them now would only cause embarrassment to the Flints. She'd made it this far, surely two more days wouldn't make that much difference.

The night of the party finally arrived. Tavia felt like a traitor as she stood in the front hall with Annie and James, dressed in her low-necked, rose-colored dress with its ruffled shirt and crinoline petticoats, meeting and greeting each guest with a pasted-on smile. Annie, who'd added more blusher to her pale cheeks than usual, looked radiant in her turquoise dress with a lovely squash-blossom necklace adorning her slim neck. James was right. She had lost weight. Despite her eyeliner and mascara, her eyes looked tired and there were dark circles under them.

Eventually, after most of the guests had arrived, the three ventured out onto the patio to join the others. Though the night was nippy, the patio was warmed by free-standing heaters the party planners had placed around the perimeter. Long strings of colored lanterns zigzagged their way overhead and thousands of tiny colored lights lit up the trees. The tables were covered with serapes in every color and laden with every Mexican food you could imagine, plus there were candles and flowers everywhere. But the highlight of it all was the gazebo, with its many strings of lights and huge crepe-paper flowers twined around its posts, fretwork and railings. It was the most magnificent thing Tavia had ever seen. Just standing there, taking it all in and watching the groups of happy people visiting and laughing together, each wearing fancy Spanish outfits, made her want to laugh and clap her hands. What a festive occasion, and it was all for her, or for who they thought she was.

"You look beautiful," someone whispered over her shoulder.

She turned quickly and looked up into the face of the most handsome man she'd ever seen. "Beck, you got your cast off!"

"Yeah, this morning. I'd hoped you were still speaking to me. I wasn't sure I should come, but James insisted, especially since I built the gazebo. I didn't want to upset him by refusing. I—I promise I'll stay away from you."

She latched on to his wrist. "No, please. I need a friend. I'm not used to being the center of attention."

James took the microphone and, with Annie by his side, thanked everyone for coming. "We're delighted to have this opportunity to introduce Jewel to all of you, our dear friends. She's become an important part of our lives."

Giving everyone a big smile, Annie took the microphone from him. "I can't begin to tell you the joy Jewel has brought into this home." Her smile disappeared as her eyes began to mist. "We will never get over the loss of our son. There'll always be a vacant spot in our hearts and lives that nothing and no one can ever fill." Annie paused and pursed her lips, fighting back tears.

Tavia, too, was fighting tears.

"But God sent Jewel to us to comfort our hearts. We love her as if she were our own daughter." Annie's smile returned and she nearly shouted, "Thank you all for coming. Enjoy yourselves. There is plenty of food. Let the party begin." Instantly the mariachi band struck up the sounds of the "Mexican Hat Dance."

By midnight, the party was over and all the guests had gone. Annie and James found places at one of the cluttered tables on the patio for one last glass of punch. "You two come and join us," James said, motioning to Tavia and Beck, who had already begun to gather up the party remains.

Though Beck seemed reluctant, Tavia tugged on his sleeve and hurried to join them, dragging him along.

"Great party, wasn't it?" James took one final swig, emptying his glass.

Annie smiled at her husband. "The very best."

"It was a nice party, sir," Beck added.

Tavia looked from one to the other. "Where's Grandpa?"

"I think he's out in the driveway, sitting in one of his girlfriend's cars, probably giving her some line of bologna. I tell you, some days, I think that man is going senile. Did you see what he had on tonight?"

Annie let out a giggle. "That's the first time I've ever seen an eighty-two-year-old man in tight troubadour pants and a red cape, with that magnificent sombrero cocked on his head. All he needed was a bull. Those girlfriends of his followed him everywhere."

"Well, I don't know about you two, but I'm bushed. I'm going to take my blushing bride of more years than I care to mention and head for bed." James reached out his hand to Annie, who took it and let him pull her to her feet. "Don't worry about the mess. The party planners are coming early in the morning to clean up."

"I'll make sure all the candles are blown out, the heaters and the lights unplugged, and all the outside doors locked before I leave, sir," Beck said, rising. "Thank you for inviting me. I enjoyed being here."

"Well, your beautiful gazebo was the hit of the party. If you have a mind to build any others, I've got at least eight friends who want one just like it. Good night."

Tavia watched them go then began moving about the patio blowing out the candles while Beck unplugged the electrical appliances, lights and heaters. Once everything was taken care of, they moved back into the house and into the foyer.

"I had a great time. Thanks for not telling the Flints about my stupid moves."

Tavia stared up into his face. "They weren't stupid moves, Beck. I'm as much to blame as you."

"Though they're still investigating the brake failure, the insurance company replaced my truck. I'm heading out with a load in the morning. I'll call you tomorrow night."

Tavia lifted her face toward Beck's, hoping for one last kiss before the truth came out, but he simply nodded his head and disappeared out the door.

Beck stared at the map as his truck barreled down the road toward California. Soon, he'd be passing the spot where the accident had happened. He slowed down as he approached the area, reliving each painful moment, especially remembering Tavia's face as she'd stared up at him from the rear window of that oversize SUV. Why was she riding in the back seat, instead of up front with her fiancé?

Once past that fateful spot, he sped up, eager to put the accident out of his mind.

By eight that night, he was checked into a cheap motel and had already eaten his supper. After staring at the phone for a number of minutes, he finally picked it up, punched in his phone-card numbers, and dialed the Flint home. Tavia answered.

"Hi, it's me."

Tavia was happy to hear Beck's voice. "Hi, Beck."

"I made my run today without any trouble, even when

I passed the spot where the accident happened. But I wondered about something. As I thought through the accident, I remembered your face looking up at me. Why were you in the back seat, instead of up front with Adam?"

She winced at his words. "I—I was tired. I wanted to—stretch out."

"I figured it was something like that. It just seemed strange. You guys being engaged and all."

"The house is back in order. The party people came early this morning and cleaned everything up."

Is she trying to change the subject?

They visited for several more minutes as he ran over the route he'd taken that day, and told her about a man he'd met at the restaurant who reminded him of Grandpa.

"You will call again, won't you?" Tavia finally asked, hating to have their conversation come to an end.

"Tomorrow night, if you're sure you want me to."

"Oh, yes, please call. I love hearing from you."

They said their goodbyes, then Beck hung up the phone, wishing he could say more.

He phoned every night that week, and sometimes they talked for as long as a half hour. The first place he went after dropping off his load that next Tuesday afternoon was to the Flint house to check on Tavia personally. She was the only one home when he arrived and she met him at the door with a smile.

"How about letting me take you into Denver for

dinner and a movie?" he asked before she could even say hello.

"The Flints are out for the evening. I'd love to go. Am I dressed okay or do I need to change?"

He gave her a quick once-over. "You look beautiful. Just right."

After a great dinner and much discussion, they decided on a movie. Since they arrived a few minutes late, they took a seat in the back and settled down with their box of popcorn, eagerly sharing it like two teenagers. It was all Beck could do to keep from putting his arm around her and pulling her close to him, but he restrained himself, knowing he had no right.

The Flints were still out when they arrived back at the house. Tavia invited Beck in for a cup of cocoa. They settled down side by side on the sofa, sipping the hot drink and laughing over the movie they'd seen. Finally Beck turned to her. "Jewel, when did you accept the Lord?"

Tavia nearly spat out her cocoa at his words. "What—what makes you ask a thing like that?"

"I just wondered. I've never heard you say how long you've been a Christian. I was curious."

She weighed her words carefully. "Would—would it surprise you if I told you I'd—I'd never been a Christian?"

He reared back with a questioning frown. "Yes, I'd be mighty surprised. You're kidding me, right? From the way the Flints talked about Adam, I assumed he wouldn't marry someone who didn't share his faith."

"That's the problem. Everyone assumed too much about me."

Beck placed his cup on the table and swiveled to face her directly. "Then you've never accepted Christ as your Savior?"

She lowered her head, avoiding his eyes. "No, I haven't, but I'd like to. I'm just not sure how to do it."

Beck reached for the Bible Annie kept on the lower shelf of the big square coffee table and turned to the book of John. "It's pretty simple, really. It says right here in God's Word, that we must confess our sins, ask for God's forgiveness, and turn our lives over to Him."

Following his finger, Tavia leaned forward and read the words. "It sounds too simple."

"God's Word is so simple a child can understand it, yet it confounds the wise." He reached out his hand to her. "Would you like to accept Christ as your Savior?"

She did a double take. "You—you mean now? I don't have to be in a church?" He gave her a smile that made her know he truly did want only the best for her.

"No, you can do it right here, right now. Would you like to kneel with me, Jewel?"

Holding on to his hand, she knelt beside him as all the sins she'd committed in her life rushed through her memory, mocking her, making her see how unworthy she was of God's love. "Are you sure He wants me?"

Beck squeezed her hand. "Oh, yes, God wants you." Beck bowed his head and asked Tavia to repeat the words after him. Though each word was agony as she thought about what she had done to the Flints, she struggled through them with tears of repentance flowing down her cheeks. When she finally rose, Beck pulled her close and told her how happy he was that she had accepted the Lord.

After answering a few more questions, Beck prayed for Tavia once more and left. As she knelt beside her bed later, she lifted her eyes toward heaven. *"God, I feel terrible even asking, but please forgive me for deceiving these wonderful people and keep them safe. Protect Annie when she finds out the truth. And, please, show me some way I can repay them. I want to make things right not only with them, but with You. I never meant any harm. And, God, thank you for Beck and his willingness to lead me to You. He's such a caring man. Be kind to him. And most of all thank you for making me see the need in my life for You.*

Though Tavia felt real peace for the first time in a long time, she knew she must set things right. Unable to face the Flints, she decided to go ahead with her original plan of leaving during the night, with notes of explanation left behind on the table. Yes, tomorrow night, while everyone is asleep, I'll leave. Before she went to bed, she penned notes to Annie, James and Grandpa, and one to Beck, then slid them under the mattress. This was what God would want her to do. As a Christian now, she knew it was God's will that she come clean and tell the truth, regardless of the cost.

Awakened by voices early the next morning, Tavia slipped into her jeans and shirt and rushed out to see what all the commotion was about.

"Annie's not feeling well," James said with great concern, his brow furrowed. "Her cardiologist is going to meet us in the emergency room of Boulder Community."

Tavia hurried to her. "What's wrong, Annie?"

Annie stared at her as if not seeing her, blinking as her eyes seemed to go in and out of focus. "Can't see you. Di-dizzy."

After throwing a blanket around her, James gathered his wife up in his arms and headed toward the door. "You and Grandpa come with me. I may need your help."

While Annie was being examined by the cardiologist and having several tests performed, James slipped his arms about Tavia and Grandpa, praying for his wife, then Grandpa prayed for her. Tavia prayed for her, too, with words that came directly from her heart.

An eternity later, the doctor appeared in the door. "We've taken a stool sample and done some blood work. Annie is bleeding internally. She has a hemoglobin level of 8.5 and melena, a darkening of stool. A gastroenterologist is going to perform a gastroscopy."

An hour later, he appeared again. "The gastroenterologist has done another test and taken a biopsy of the site of the bleeding and has sent it to the lab for analysis. Annie has been bleeding internally from an ulcer caused by *H. pylori* bacteria, which can be treated with a course of antibiotics. She's been sedated. It'll be a while before the effects wear off."

"Can—can I sit with her?" Tavia asked, terrified by the seriousness of the doctor's report.

The man shrugged. "Fine with me. I'm sure she'll be glad to find you there when she wakes up." He turned to James. "We're admitting her. She's lost a lot of blood and is going to have to have a transfusion. We'll give her two units of packed cells and keep her overnight for observation. I want to make sure she's closely monitored for any signs of congestive heart failure since she has a weak heart." A nurse hurried up to him and spoke to him in soft tones.

He turned to them with a frown. "I'm told Annie has antibodies to the AB blood that's on hand. They're going to put out a call from the blood bank for more AB blood. I'm not sure how long it will take before we find some that Annie's body will accept."

"I have AB blood," Tavia said excitedly, grabbing on to the doctor's sleeve. "They told me when I was in the hospital after the accident. Can I give her my blood?"

The doctor smiled at her. "Your blood may not work, either, but it's worth a try. Come with me."

Thirty minutes later, the doctor walked into the little sterile room wearing a broad smile and said, "Your blood is compatible with Annie's."

"Please let me be the donor. It's one small way I can repay Annie for her kindness to me."

James wrapped his arm about her shoulders. "Oh, Jewel, you have no idea how much I appreciate this."

"Me, too," Grandpa added. "We have to do all we can for our little Annie."

After the transfusion, Tavia was allowed to spend the night sitting in the hospital room with Annie. At Annie's request, James was getting some much-needed rest on a couch in the waiting room. Just watching the rhythmic rise and fall of Annie's chest as she slept made her feel good, and she thanked the Lord for the privilege of allowing her to give her blood to this lovely woman who had endured so much and done it with such grace. During the middle of the night, Annie whispered to her, "Jewel, do you realize your blood is flowing through my veins? Now, we're more than just almost mother-in-law and almost daughter-in-law. We're real family." With that, she turned her head away and drifted back to sleep.

Two weeks passed, and although Annie was getting stronger by the day, she still had to take things easy and rest as much as possible. Tavia prayed constantly that she would recover. Each day Beck was in town, he came to the Flints to check on Annie, and on the days he wasn't on the road, he phoned. Though they both shied away from talking about what had happened between them, he and Tavia talked for hours about many subjects, from politics to sports, to the weather and foods they liked. She loved talking to him. His voice was always gentle and filled with concern for both her and Annie.

"The doctor says I'm doing fine now," Annie told Tavia, returning from an appointment with her physician. "He gave me an all-clear."

Though Tavia smiled, her heart was breaking. The time for her to leave had finally come again. While Annie was taking her afternoon nap, she packed a few things in a box and carried it out to her car, placing it in the trunk so it wouldn't be discovered. Though she still hated the idea of taking the car, it would be next to impossible to get a Denver taxi to come all the way up into the foothills to pick her up. Besides, taking the car would allow her to leave at whatever time during the night worked out best. After going back into the house, she went to her room and pulled the notes she had written from beneath the mattress, rereading them to make sure they said exactly what she wanted to say, adding a few things here and there.

Dinner that night was difficult for her as she scanned each smiling face around the table. Beck was in town so he was there, too. Even Grandpa was at home. She wanted to remember this moment forever, to etch it in her mind. These were the people she loved more than anyone else on earth. The only real family she'd ever had, and they weren't even hers. With great effort, she fought back tears and kept on a happy face.

When Beck rose to go, she walked him to his car and knowing she shouldn't, but unable to resist, slipped her arms about his neck and kissed him. At first, he seemed shocked by her unexpected action and simply stared at her, but it didn't take long for him to respond, wrapping his arms about her and drawing her close to him.

"I love you, Beck. Remember that, no matter what happens," she whispered in his ear, her hand caressing his broad neck.

He leaned back slightly and gave her a frown. "What does that mean?"

She twined her fingers through his hair. "Please say you love me, too. Even if you don't mean it. I need to hear it."

"I—I do love you. I've already told you that." He gave her a mystified look. "What's going on?"

"Nothing you need be concerned about." She pulled free of his arms and took a few steps backward, her eyes still fixed on his. "Goodbye, Beck. You're a very special man. Knowing you has been a wonderful experience."

Again, he gave her a puzzled look. "You make that goodbye sound so—final."

She blew him a kiss then hurried into the house, closing the door behind her, leaning against it as she heard the lock engage, her heart broken. Turning her back on this man, the one true love of her life, was even harder than she'd imagined.

When she entered the family room, James, Annie and Grandpa were sitting in front of the TV watching the local news. Tavia said good-night to them, making sure to kiss each man on the cheek and give Annie an extra-special kiss and hug, then headed toward her bedroom, planning to wait until they were asleep before leaving. She would be heading back to Denver or maybe even Colorado Springs; at this point she hadn't decided which.

Several hours later, hoping the rest of the household was sound asleep, Tavia moved cautiously out of her room and into the family room. Removing the engagement ring from her finger, she carefully placed her notes on the coffee table with the ring resting on top, adding the credit card and the bankbook, from which she'd withdrawn no money. Inside her purse she carried the ten-dollar bill Jewel had given her, and the seven hundred dollars James had insisted she take when she'd arrived at their house. She left an IOU for the amount on top of the checkbook. On top of the bankbook, she arranged Adam's baby ring and the gold chain. After lining them up carefully, she moved stealthily toward the door with only her purse, jacket and the Bible Beck had given her in hand.

With one last look at the home she had shared with the Flints for such a brief time, she backed quietly out the door, closing it securely behind her. By the time anyone discovered she was gone, she hoped, she would have left her Mercedes parked along some Denver or

Colorado Springs street. She'd leave it locked, with the Flints' name and phone number on the front seat and her set of keys under the mat. By the time police responded to her call about an abandoned car, she'd be miles away. Since no one actually knew who she was or where she'd come from, maybe, just maybe, she wouldn't be found.

Chapter Thirteen

Annie's shrill scream awakened the entire household.

"Annie! What is it? What's wrong?" James rushed into the family room, wild-eyed, hair askew, an overnight growth of beard darkening his cheeks and chin, and hooked his arm about his wife's waist.

"Jewel's dead!"

Rubbing his eyes, Grandpa, dressed in plaid flannel pajamas hurried up beside them, clamping a hand on his son's arm.

"Jewel's dead?" James glanced around quickly then lifted Annie's face to his, his brows angled upward with concern. "Annie! You have to calm down. You're not making any sense! What do you mean— Jewel's dead? Where is she? She was fine when we went to bed!"

Annie's body shook violently as she gasped for air.

"The woman we thought was Jewel wasn't Jewel at all! She's gone! She left this note, along with the engagement ring and Adam's baby ring and chain and the bankbook and credit card you'd given her," she screeched at him, shoving the note into his hands. "She left one for Beck, too."

"I'd better call Beck." Grandpa moved quickly toward the phone.

James grabbed the note from his hysterical wife's hand and began to read it aloud.

"Dearest Annie, James and Grandpa,
Before you read this note, I want you to remember one thing. I love each one of you more than I've ever loved anyone. I know that's going to be hard to believe after you hear what I am about to tell you, but it's true. You're the first real family I have ever had."

James stared down at Annie. "What is this?"

Annie rubbed at her forehead, still stunned by the words. "She lied to us!"

James's hand trembled as he once again lifted the note.

"Beck is on his way," Grandpa said, putting a steadying hand on James's shoulder.

James's eyes probed Annie's face for a moment then he continued to read.

"I have a confession to make before I begin my story. I am not who you think I am. My name is Tavia MacRae, not Jewel. The real Jewel is dead."

Annie grabbed on to her husband's arm for support as she burst into tears. "Oh, James, this doesn't make any sense! Where *is* Jewel?"

Grandpa rubbed at the stubble on his chin. "She's not Jewel? How can that be?"

"I don't know, Dad." James met his wife's worried eyes. "If what she's saying is true, what was she doing in Adam's truck?"

"She's dead! Jewel is dead!" Annie let out a gasp, her hands going to cover her mouth. James quickly grabbed on to her arm and led her to the sofa, gently lowering her onto it before seating himself beside her, his troubled eyes scanning her face. "Are you sure you want to hear the rest of this, sweetheart? Your health is more important than anything that could be written in this note."

Annie felt breathless and her pulse raced as she linked her arm through her husband's and leaned her head onto his shoulder. "I—I have to hear it, James!"

James watched her for a second and then continued to read.

"I hardly know where to begin. I guess at the very beginning. I was working as a waitress in Denver when I met this really handsome man. He seemed nice enough, so when he invited me to take a drive with him up into the mountains near Glenwood Springs to get some money a friend of his owed him, I accepted. After we'd driven several hours he pulled the car down an exit ramp and onto a side road, then parked and tried to—well—you know. I fought him off and he got really angry and called me all sorts of names. After slapping and hitting me a few times, he pushed me out, then drove off and left me there, taking my jacket and purse with him."

Annie nervously bit her lip. "What is she trying to say? And what does any of this have to do with us?"

James shrugged. "I don't understand, either."

Grandpa lowered himself onto the sofa beside them and peeled off his glasses. "Go on, James. Read the rest."

"I walked back onto the highway and tried desperately to get someone to stop and give me a ride into the next town, but it seemed everyone was afraid to pick up a hitchhiker. Until your son came along."

Annie buried her face in her hands. "Oh, Adam!"

"He didn't want to pick up a hitchhiker, but Jewel felt sorry for me and begged him to stop. After I explained what had happened he offered me a ride to where I could call someone."

"The woman we thought was Jewel was a hitch-hiker?" Annie said, clutching on to James's arm even more tightly.

"It's beginning to sound that way." James stared at the paper.

"Adam and Jewel were so nice to me. They told me all about themselves, how they'd met and fallen in love. They even told me you'd never seen a photograph of Jewel. You would have loved Jewel, Annie. And she would have loved you. Like me, Jewel had no family and was so looking forward to becoming a part of yours. She was wildly in love with your son and one of the sweetest women I have ever met, and she loved her engagement ring—the one you gave Adam to give to her. She insisted I try it on. She said it made her feel like a queen. I really didn't want to. I was afraid of dropping it and not being able to find it. That's the way my luck usually runs. Nothing but trouble. But she kept insisting, so finally I put it on. That's when Beck's truck began bearing down on us. We were all so frightened, all we could think about was that truck coming up so rapidly behind us. Then it hit us! That was the last thing

I remembered until I woke up in the hospital and all of you were hovering over me."

"What about Jewel?" Annie inserted quickly. "If she isn't Jewel, where is Adam's fiancée?"

Grandpa pressed his eyelids shut tightly. "I'm not sure we want to know."

"I had no idea who any of you were, and with that tube down my throat there was no way I could ask you. I couldn't even manage to write you a note with an IV in one hand and a cast on the other. At first, I thought you had the wrong room. Then, after I finally realized you were Adam's parents, I figured he had been injured, too, and had sent you to check on me. Then you began to call me Jewel and I went into shock. I had no idea Jewel hadn't been found. By that time, I had heard everyone talking over and over about Annie's heart condition, and how glad you were that I had survived. Rather, I should say Jewel had survived.

The same day Annie brought me the pretty nightgowns and robe, James told me Adam had died in the accident. I couldn't believe it. He was such a wonderful person. I was sick over it, and I felt so sorry for the three of you. When there was no mention of Jewel I suddenly realized since no one knew Adam had picked up a hitchhiker, everyone had assumed *I* was Jewel. No one had even looked for her! I was in agony. I wanted to tell you, but couldn't.

Then that state trooper who worked the accident stopped by my room to visit with Grandpa and told him there was no way anyone who had been in that SUV could have survived, the way it rolled end over end down into that canyon. At that moment, I knew Jewel had died, too."

Annie's mouth went suddenly dry. "No wonder she gave us such a bewildered look every time we called her Jewel!"

"She had no right to deceive us that way," James ground out, his face hardening. "Just think what she put us all through. And poor Jewel. Her body is still lying out there somewhere."

"Maybe her intent was to protect you." Grandpa steepled his hands in front of his face contemplatively. "We're the ones who assumed she was Jewel. She never once actually told us that's who she was. Try putting yourself in her place. She was dazed, injured pretty badly, had just come out of a coma and found herself in a strange place, being hovered over by people she didn't know. Think, James, how many times did we tell her how glad we were she was alive, and what it would have done to us, especially Annie, if she had died, too."

"But, Dad, she wasn't Jewel, she—"

Heartbroken and feeling deceived, Annie tugged on James's sleeve. "You're right, James. That woman lied to us. Not only that, she forced her way into our lives! Into our home!"

Grandpa gave his head a shake. "No, we're the ones who did the forcing. Not once did she ask to be brought into this home. We made that decision for her. All three of us." He gestured toward the note in his son's hand. "Read the rest of it, James. Let's see what else she has to say."

"There is no excuse for what she has done!" James sent his father a look of exasperation before going on.

"Then James came to the hospital late that night and told me Adam's funeral was to be the next day, and how worried he was about Annie—whether she'd be strong enough to make it through the service. I wanted to tell him then, but I would never have forgiven myself if the truth, coming from my lips, had sent Annie into a fatal heart attack. I never meant to deceive anyone, honest I didn't, but you all had me so scared."

Annie sucked in several restorative breaths in an attempt to settle down, determined to keep her heart under control.

"Then you began to talk about bringing me here to your lovely home and nursing me back to health. As much as I needed a place to go, I didn't want to let that happen. I felt dreadful about accepting your help, but what else could I do? I thought about trying to get dressed and slip out of the hospital, but I didn't even have clothes. You'd brought them home with you. The only money I'd had with me was the ten-dollar bill Jewel had given me to call someone to come for me and to get a bite to eat, and it was here at your house, too, in the pocket of my jeans. I had no place to go. No one to call. I didn't know what to do. And I was so worried about Jewel it was making me ill. I couldn't eat. I couldn't sleep for worrying about it. I know that's no excuse. What I did was wrong—very wrong."

Both anger and compassion flowed through Annie as she listened to Tavia's words. Her heart did go out to this woman and what she'd been through as the result of the accident, yet was any of that reason enough to do what she had done?

"I know you've probably been confused about my reactions to Beck. Again, I'll have to be honest with you. I've never met a man like Beck. In so many ways, he reminds me of your Adam. Kind, caring and so very thoughtful. The way he sat patiently by me all those days at the hospital, praying for me like he did, well, it touched me deeply, and I found myself looking forward to his visits. He was everything I've always thought the perfect husband should be, and before I knew it, I'd fallen deeply in love with him. Please don't blame any of this on Beck. He was only there because he was concerned about me and felt the accident was his fault. I never told him the truth."

James gave his fingers a loud snap. "At times, I kind of suspected there was something going on between those two, but I couldn't understand why Jewel would have any interest in another man that quickly. Knowing Adam, and how particular he'd been about the women he'd dated, it just didn't make sense."

Annie pressed her fingers to her temples. "Do you think she's telling the truth about Beck?"

James huffed. "I'd like to think so. I really like that guy, but he's sure been interested in her."

Grandpa's brows furrowed into a scowl. "Don't you think you should read the rest of her note before you jump to any more conclusions?"

"Yeah, Dad, you're probably right." James gave Annie a concerned look then turned to the next page of the letter.

"I know this note is long and I apologize for it, but these are the things I needed to tell you—things it was only right that you should hear. If I'd had my way, I would have told you the minute I came out of that coma that I wasn't Jewel, but because of my injuries and my limited movement, it was impossible. I never asked for any of this. I was a victim of circumstances, too. Just like Adam and Jewel, I was in the wrong place at the wrong time."

James rubbed the back of his neck, then read on.

"Though you may not think so, something good has come out of all of this turmoil and deception. At least, good for me. Because of the life Beck and the three of you have lived before me, I realized I was a sinner and needed to get myself right with God. Not only because of the sin I was committing by keeping the truth from you, but the sins I've committed all my life. My background has been pretty ugly and I'm ashamed of it. I wanted to know God like the four of you know Him, but I didn't know how, and I wasn't sure God would even be interested in someone like me. Finally, the night of the party, I admitted to Beck that I wasn't a Christian."

Annie felt a flush rise to her face. "James! Remember how embarrassed she was the first time you asked her to pray? I thought it was because she was nervous about praying in front of us. Adam had told us Jewel had been a Christian since she was a very young girl. I have to admit I was surprised by her simple prayer, but at the time I never gave it much thought."

"I thought her prayer was kind of sweet," Grandpa added, his voice gritty with emotion.

"Did you ever have any suspicions, Dad?" James asked bluntly.

"Not exactly suspicions. It kind of surprised me that she didn't talk about Adam much, so one evening after you two had gone to bed, I asked her about it. She didn't give me a direct answer, but she mentioned the time he ruined his mother's brownies and a couple of other things that had happened. After that, I felt bad for even mentioning it. Maybe we all overlooked the obvious because we wanted so badly to believe Adam's fiancée hadn't died in the accident."

Annie's body sagged as a sudden sting of tears flowed down her cheeks. "I have to admit I loved having her around. Oh, James, we had so much fun together. Having her here was not only like having a bit of Adam with us, it was like having the daughter we lost." Annie's flow of tears turned into a flood. "I can't tell you how much her confession upsets me. I loved that girl like she was my own."

James cuddled her close and gently kissed her forehead. "I'm sorry, Annie." He offered a sheepish grin. "I—I hate to admit it, but I loved her, too."

"So did I!" Grandpa leaned against the arm of the sofa and clasped his gnarled fingers together. "Although I find it hard to condone what she's done, in all honesty, I have no idea what I would have done if I'd been in her place."

James nodded. "I gave her that bankbook, made several sizable deposits into her account, set up a credit card in her name, even gave her a large sum of cash. Yet—" He rose and spread out the pile of things on the table. "She never used any of them, and she's left an IOU for the seven hundred dollars she took with her. That sure doesn't sound like she was out to bilk us."

"What about the car?" Grandpa asked.

James shrugged. "She had to have taken it. How else would she leave?"

Annie gestured toward him. "Read the rest, James."

"Okay. She says,

'I told Beck I really wanted to let God take over my life, but I didn't know how. He told me how simple it was, and that night, I knelt by your fireplace and asked God's forgiveness and turned my life over to him.'"

Annie sniffled, overcome by the words. "Oh, James, At least she got herself right with the Lord before she left. Do you suppose God sent her into our lives so she could be saved?"

His brow furrowed slightly. "I find it hard to believe God would take the lives of two young people with such promising futures as our Adam and Jewel to reach her. He could have found an easier way."

"Are you saying you know better than God?" Grandpa asked in a kindly fashion.

James paused, stuffing his free hand into his pocket and staring at the floor. "Of course not. I'm sorry, Dad, I didn't mean to sound so pompous, but I miss Adam. He was my only son."

"God sent His only son to die for the sins of anyone who would accept Him. Not just you or Annie, or me, or even Adam. He died for this young woman, too."

"He did, James," Annie said softly, feeling some of the same emotions as her husband. "But why Adam? Why Jewel, instead of someone else? Adam has been our life, and he's gone. And so is his fiancée, the daughter we finally thought we had. But Grandpa is right. God works in mysterious ways, His wonders to perform." She stiffened, lifting her tearstained face to her husband. "But why hasn't anyone found Jewel's body?" She shuddered at the thought of that beautiful young woman lying somewhere out in that canyon.

James swallowed hard as his thumb wiped at her tears. "I don't know, sweetheart. Probably because no one has even considered she was there."

"What else does she say?" Grandpa prodded, his own eyes filling with tears.

"She goes on to say," James read, not realizing how deeply the disturbing questions were preying on Annie's mind.

"This is so hard to explain on paper. Annie, I hope my words haven't sent your weak heart into a tail-spin. Please be careful and take care of yourself. You are so important to so many who love you. Though I'm sure you don't care, you're important to me. I cherish the day you asked me to call you Mother. My own mother died when I was two. I never knew the true meaning of the word *mother,* or what a mother should be to her child until I met you. I'll hold on to the moments I spent with you forever."

I'll hold on to them too, Annie said in her heart.

"I was going to leave earlier. I had this note all written, my belongings gathered, and was ready to leave as soon as you and James were asleep, but that was the evening we had to rush you to the hospital. We were afraid you wouldn't live, then I was allowed to give you my blood. You can't believe how excited I was finally to have something I could do for you. Not that giving my blood could in any way make up for what I have done. I knew it couldn't, but it was all I had to offer you."

Annie closed her eyes and gulped hard. Grandpa reached across the sofa to pat her arm. "How are you doing, Annie-girl?"

She gave him a weak smile. "Surprisingly well, Dad—considering all that's happened."

"You sure you want me to go on?" James asked, holding out the letter.

Annie nodded. "Yes, I want to hear it all."

"As soon as the doctor said you were doing better and your health had seemed to stabilize, I decided it was time for me to leave. I packed my things, deciding to leave tonight while the three of you were sleeping. I'm driving the Mercedes. I thought about calling for a taxi, but since there isn't one available way out here, I'm taking the Mercedes. As soon as I get to my destination, I'll leave a note on the seat with your phone number, saying it belongs to you and call it in to the police as an abandoned car. I know, as Christians, you will see that Jewel gets the Christian burial she deserves, and that gives me great comfort."

"Of course we will!" Annie burst out in tears. "What turmoil must have been going on inside that young woman. I almost feel sorry for her. Do you think the authorities will try to find her and prosecute her for this?"

Her husband pinched the bridge of his nose with his thumb and forefinger. "I honestly don't know what they'll do, Annie."

Grandpa swiveled in his seat to face his son. "They'd only know about it if you filed charges. Are you going to?"

Annie's hand went to her mouth. "Oh, James, do you think we should?"

His brows climbed his forehead. "She needs to pay for what she's done."

"She's already been through so much."

"But is that enough? Through her silence, a young woman's body has been lying out in that canyon for weeks."

Grandpa let out a long sigh. "Should we be punished for assuming she was Jewel?"

"But, Dad—"

The old man put a hand on his son's arm. "There is much to consider before any decision is made. I think we'd better give this a little more thought before doing anything as rash as talking about filing charges. Maybe you should talk to your attorney, James."

James leaned back against the sofa, his palms flattened against his face. "You're probably right. All of this has hit us so fast, I'm sure we each need time to think things over, but I'll call my attorney, then call the sheriff. He'll want to organize a search party to find Jewel's body."

Annie gave him a gentle nudge with her elbow. "Is there more?"

"Yeah, there is." He sat up straight and flipped to the next page.

"Leaving the three of you and Beck is the hardest thing I have ever done. I love all of you. Yes, I love Beck, too. I can't begin to tell you how much. He means everything to me, but I have never been able to tell him, since, like you, he has always assumed I was Jewel. At times, I thought he was beginning to love me too, but I knew he would never be able love me as Jewel, because he knew how much Jewel loved Adam. And he'd never be able to love me as Tavia MacRae, the liar. He could never tolerate that, or accept it. For me, living a life with Beck was hopeless. He's too fine a man and has too much love for God even to begin to think about spending his life with me, but I'll always be grateful for the way he has been so patient with me and led me to his Lord. Please, never for one moment, think Beck ever knew the truth."

"That's a relief," Grandpa said, pushing his glasses up his nose a notch. "I've always thought of Beck as a fine man."

James nodded his head in agreement. "Me, too, Dad."

"I—I feel so sorry for her. For both of them. What if Beck loves her like she loves him?" Annie added.

James frowned. "Loves? From the way her note

sounds, the two of them haven't even had a chance to get acquainted. How could they love each other?"

Annie lifted her face and kissed her husband's cheek. "Like the two of us did, James. Have you forgotten? We were smitten with each other the first day we met. I knew then you were the only person I'd ever love. You told me you felt the same way."

The sound of a car in the driveway brought their conversation to a halt.

Chapter Fourteen

Beck raced up onto the front porch and pressed the doorbell, waiting impatiently until George Flint's face appeared. "What's up? Why did you want me to come over? Is Annie okay?"

Grandpa gave his head a sad shake as he closed the door. "I'd better let Annie and James explain."

James extended his hand. "I'm glad you came right over, Beck. She left a note for you."

Beck's heart dropped with an inaudible thud. "Jewel's gone? Where?"

James cupped his fingers around Beck's upper arm. "Jewel—well, not Jewel, but—"

Annie rose quickly to stand by her husband. "Maybe you'd better give him his note."

James moved to the table, took the note and handed it to Beck.

"I don't understand. What is this?"

Annie tugged on the big man's arm. "You'd better sit down before you read it."

Doing as she suggested, he settled himself on the sofa, then opened the envelope and began to read.

Dearest Beck,
I've been carrying a terrible secret. It's time I told you the truth. I am not Jewel Mallory.

Beck felt his world collapse. "Is this some kind of joke?" He looked from Annie to James to Grandpa. "I don't get it. What's going on? Where is she?"

James gestured toward the note. "Go ahead. Read it. I'm sure her note will explain everything. She left one for us, too."

Beck stared at the words on the paper.

I am not Jewel Mallory. I am Tavia MacRae, a hitchhiker Adam and Jewel picked up along the highway after my date shoved me out of his car and left me stranded with no way to get home and no money.

"Tavia MacRae? Why did she let everyone think she was Jewel?" Beck nearly shouted out, his hands trembling as he held the note.

"It was our fault." Grandpa stepped forward. "She

never told us that's who she was. The poor girl was in a coma. We all assumed she was Jewel because she was wearing the engagement ring Annie had given Adam to give to Jewel."

Beck shook his head, trying to make sense of things. "Why was she wearing Jewel's ring?"

"Because Jewel insisted she try it on," Annie explained. "Then the accident happened and that woman was thrown from Adam's truck as it went over the guardrail. When we saw her at the hospital and she had the ring on, we all thought she was Jewel."

Beck felt his heart sink like a rock tossed into a pond. "So the woman we all knew as Jewel was not Jewel, but a stranger?"

James reached out a hand to his wife. "Why don't we go in the kitchen and let Beck read his note in privacy? I could sure use a good strong cup of coffee."

Grandpa bobbed his head. "I think we could all use a good strong cup of coffee."

"You don't have to leave—"

"We know," Annie said, taking James's hand. "But it might be best if you had time to read the entire note through before we all talk this thing over and decide what to do and where to go from here. Call us when you're finished."

The three moved toward the kitchen as Beck, confused and upset, nodded, lowered his gaze and continued to read.

Before I go any further, I must tell you I have loved you almost from the day you came into my hospital room carrying that teddy bear.

"You love me?" Beck asked aloud, her words startling him. "Then how could you let me think you were someone else?"

You were so sweet I wanted to throw my arms around your neck and kiss you. That bear and the Bible you gave me are the only possessions I have now.

Beck leaned back against the sofa's soft cushions, his mind awhirl.

I never intended to deceive you, Beck, but I was caught up in circumstances beyond my control. For some unknown reason, God allowed me to live and took Adam and Jewel. I can't begin to understand His reasoning. I'm a nobody. My life could have been snuffed out and no one would have missed me. But since you've led me to the Lord, I've learned I am important to God. He has inscribed my name on the palms of His hands.

Beck stared at the words. Yes, he was thankful he'd had the opportunity to lead this young woman to Christ, but still felt betrayed. "But, Jewel, or Tavia, or whatever your name is—how could you deceive me, too?" he asked aloud, his anger rising as his fingers tightly clutched the paper. "Especially, if you loved me as you say you do?"

He read on, carefully assessing Tavia's recounting of events, his emotions a roller-coaster ride of highs and lows.

When he came to the final paragraph, he paused, his heart heavy.

So, my dearest Beck, I have no other choice but to leave. I deserve any punishment the law or Annie and James decide to give me. There is no doubt in my mind that they will be able to find me if they choose to file some sort of charges against me.

As much as I'd like to, I won't even ask for your forgiveness, but I do ask you to try and remember the wonderful times we had together. I can't thank you enough for each one of them. Perhaps in another time—in another place—the two of us could have gotten together. That would have been the dream of a lifetime.

So goodbye, Beck. You are always in my heart and my thoughts. I love you now, and I'll love you always.

Beck stared at the signature. Tavia MacRae. The words were foreign to him. Despite the hurt and anger that coursed through him, he had to admit he loved the woman who had written that note, loved her with a love he'd never felt for anyone else. But even if she hadn't run away would he have ever been able to forgive her for what she had done?

"I brought you a cup of hot coffee."

Still lost in thought, Beck started at the sound of Annie's voice.

"I didn't mean to disturb you."

He folded Tavia's note and slipped it into his jacket pocket. "It's okay. I'm finished."

"I'm sure you were as surprised as we were," James said as he came into the room with Grandpa at his heels.

Beck nodded. "I don't know what to say."

James sat down on the sofa and tugged his wife down beside him, then motioned Beck and Grandpa to the two club chairs opposite them. "I think the four of us need to discuss this thing and then decide what we should do next."

Chapter Fifteen

❧

The first thing Tavia did after abandoning the car in Denver was to take a bus to Colorado Springs, trying to put as much distance as possible between herself and the Flints. Then it was time to look for a job. Though none of the first four restaurants she applied to needed any help, the fifth one hired her. After that, she located a cheap one-room furnished apartment within walking distance of the restaurant and unpacked the few items she'd brought with her. The place was dingy and poorly lit, smelled of stale tobacco smoke and had traces of mouse droppings. Not at all like the home she'd been living in up in the Denver foothills, but it would do. It had to.

She longed to hear whether Jewel's body had been located yet, but purchasing a radio or TV was out of the question. It'd taken well over half of the money she had with her just to pay for her bus ride to Colorado Springs, her rent, and to purchase towels and sheets. Fortunately, she was allowed to eat one meal at the restaurant each day she worked so she wouldn't be buying much food. One meal a day would have to suffice.

Though her job was demanding, she liked the people she worked with. Some of the other waitresses had bigger problems, with kids to support on that salary. Maybe, she decided, once she'd paid the seven hundred dollars back to the Flints she'd be able to enroll in night school. Maybe train in medical records or as a nurse's aide—if the Flints or the law didn't come looking for her to make restitution for what she had done.

Each day she trudged to work, stood on her feet all day then trudged back home to her empty apartment, finding her only solace and encouragement in her Bible. Although she was by herself, she wasn't alone. She had the Lord with her now, and for that she'd be forever grateful to the Flints and to Beck. Each of them had been an example of God's love. She took special pleasure in the snapshots Annie had taken the night of the party and had duplicated for Tavia. There was even one of her and Beck together. How happy they looked as they'd smiled at the camera that night. But the picture she loved best was the one Annie had taken of Beck in his black velvet sombrero. He looked so handsome with it cocked low on his brow and his crooked, mischievous smile. Just looking at it made her want to laugh, though laughs were few and far between.

At the end of the second week, as Tavia was walking toward the restaurant, she glanced up and caught sight of a huge picture of herself on a billboard along the side of the road. Startled, she stopped and stared at it. It was one of the pictures Annie had taken of her the night of the party. Under the picture in big bold letters it read, Come Home. We love you. All is forgiven. Mom, Dad, Grandpa and Beck.

Tavia couldn't believe her eyes. Could this really be happening? How had her hiding place been discovered so soon?

Wanting to return, but afraid if she did return the authorities might prosecute her for impersonating Jewel, she reluctantly turned her back on the sign and went on to work, trying to put it out of her mind.

Several times that day, as customers came in and out of the restaurant, a number of them commented how much she looked like the girl they'd seen on a billboard. Some of them said they had seen more billboards on the opposite side of town, and Tavia realized the same picture and message must be up all over Colorado Springs. As she walked home from work that night, she paused to look intently at the billboard once again. What if she called them from a pay phone and stayed on only a few minutes? Would they be able to trace the call?

She ached to get in touch with the Flints, to see if the promise of the message was true, but how could she? As she passed the pay phone in the lobby of her apartment house, she stopped and stood staring at it for a long time. Finally, she emptied her day's tips onto the little shelf beneath the phone and placed the call.

James answered on the first ring. "Oh, Tavia, where are you? We've been frantic!"

Tears rolled down her cheeks at the sound of his voice. "How—how's Annie? Is she all right?"

"I'm here, Tavia, on the extension phone."

Tavia breathed a sigh of relief. Praise God, Annie is alive. "I—I never meant to deceive you, honest I didn't. It all happened so fast and everyone thought I was Jewel, and I had that thing in my throat—"

"We understand," James said kindly. "It was more our fault than yours. We realize that now. Everyone at the hospital and the four of us just assumed you were Jewel and put you in an untenable position."

Tavia began to cry uncontrollably, making it difficult to form her words. "You—you and the doctor were talking about Annie, and I—"

"We know, Tavia. We understand." Annie's voice was gentle and bore no malice. "Oh, we were all pretty angry when we began to read your letter, but we had to admit you never once told us outright that you were Jewel, and you didn't take anything from us, so we knew you weren't out to take what you could from us. Once we sat down and talked about it rationally, we realized your place is here with us now. We want you to come home."

Come home? Next to hearing Beck say he loved her even if he hadn't meant it, those were the sweetest words she'd ever heard.

"Hi, my little sweetie. Your room is waiting for you."

A smile swept across Tavia's face. "Grandpa? Is that you?"

"Yep, it's me all right. Come home, darlin'. We Flints need you. Hang on, there's someone else here who wants to speak to you."

"Hi, Tavia. It's me. Beck."

Her heart did cartwheels at the sound of his voice. "Beck?"

"We all want you to come home, Tavia. I've been miserable not knowing where you are. I love you. I thought I'd die when I lost you."

Tavia closed her eyes and pressed her forehead against the wall. "But after your fiancée lied to you about having been married before, you said you could never love a woman who lied to you."

"I never thought I could, but I realized my own part in this mishap." Beck paused. "God has forgiven you, Tavia, I have to do the same thing."

Tavia felt as if the great weight that had been pressing against her chest had been lifted. "You mean that? You forgive me?"

"Yes, I forgive you. I've prayed about this, Tavia. God has spoken to my heart. He's spoken to my heart about something else, too. I'll tell you when I see you."

Hesitant to hear what else he had to say, yet jubilant that he could forgive her, Tavia pressed the phone closer to her ear.

"I love you, Tavia MacRae."

"I love you, too, Beck. I can't tell you how much I've missed you."

"We have so much to talk about, I can hardly wait to see you. I have to give the phone to James now. Remember, I love you, sweetheart."

Tavia found herself speechless. Never had she expected things to turn out this way.

"Tell me where you are and I'll leave immediately to come for you," James said.

Still unable to believe this was happening and stammering for words, Tavia gave him the address of her apartment and directions on how to get there. Long after he had hung up the phone, she was still standing in the lobby staring at the receiver. Had this all been a dream or had it really happened? In a few hours she'd know. James had said he was on the way.

The ride from Colorado Springs to the Flints' was pleasant but seemed to take forever. Tavia was so anxious to see Beck and Annie and Grandpa she could hardly stand the wait. James told her how much Beck had wanted to come with him, but he'd asked him to stay behind with Annie and Grandpa. With Annie's health, he never knew when she might need to be driven to the hospital.

Tavia's excitement nearly overwhelmed her as James turned the car through the iron gates and up the circle drive in front of the house. There, on a big sign stretched over the front door, emblazoned in huge letters, were the words, Welcome Home, Daughter. Tears gushed forth, momentarily blinding her. Annie, Grandpa and Beck all rushed out the door, running to meet her, all three hugging her at once.

Once they were all inside and the excitement had calmed down a bit, they settled themselves onto the sofa and into the chairs in front of the fireplace, Tavia's most loved spot in the house.

"I was so afraid of what the shock might do to Annie when she found my note," Tavia confessed shyly.

James wrapped an arm about his wife and pulled her close. "She's taken it surprisingly well, haven't you, sweetheart?"

She nodded as she nestled into his side.

"We had quite a discussion with Beck after we read your note," James said. "He admitted he'd kissed you."

"When I told him, I thought he was going to deck me," Beck volunteered with a glance toward James. "I deserved it. I had no right, not when I thought you were Jewel, but I had to tell him."

James cocked a brow as he gave Beck a smile. "But there was a sincerity in his eyes that made us understand what he had done. He apologized and admitted he'd loved you since he'd visited you in the hospital. Coming to know Beck like we had, we realized his heart had momentarily overruled his good sense." James nodded toward Annie. "I have to be honest. Annie was engaged to another man when I met her. I should have done the gentlemanly thing and left her alone but, like Beck, I fell head over heels for that pretty little gal the minute I saw her and I did everything I could to break them up. Eventually, it worked, but I was never very proud of myself for what I had done."

Annie leaned her head on her husband's shoulder and smiled up at him. "Looking back, I'm convinced the two of us getting together was God's will. I can't imagine sharing this many years with anyone else."

James nodded in agreement. "After we read your note, we decided to pray about it and let the Lord handle it. It was too much for us mere mortals to understand."

Annie nodded at James's words. "At first, we thought about pressing charges, but we realized you hadn't actually done anything illegal. At least, not unless the authorities can file charges against you for not telling us about Jewel when you were finally able to talk."

"You probably could have told us who you were when they took that tube out of your throat," Grandpa chimed in, "but by then we had you so anxious about what it would do to Annie if she lost you, you probably thought you were doing us a favor by keeping quiet."

"I had been concerned about something from the very beginning," Beck confessed, rising and pacing about the room. "I remembered seeing your face peering up at me from that back seat and it haunted me. Why would an engaged woman be sitting in the back seat instead of up front with her fiancé? But you'd said you wanted to stretch out and rest." He bent toward her, bracing his hand on the arm of the sofa. "With that doubt aside, I still couldn't accept I'd kissed a woman who had so recently lost the love of her life. And how could she kiss me back? You can't believe the guilt I felt."

Tavia stared at him, too much in shock even to respond. James saw her shock and changed the subject.

"You were right there with us the night Annie got sick and had to be rushed to the hospital," James said. "But because of you, Annie came out of her sickness much faster than the doctor thought she would, and I was so grateful to you. Then you disappeared." James let out a sigh. "We thought we'd lost you forever." He waved a hand toward Beck. "It was Beck's idea to put up the billboards. He figured you would either go to Denver or Colorado Springs."

Tavia gaped at them. The cost had to be astronomical. "You put them up in both cities?"

Beck nodded. "We figured even if you didn't see them, perhaps someone who recognized you would, and would tell you about them."

"No one realized Jewel had died or suspected you'd been a hitchhiker until we read your note," Annie said, her fingers stroking Tavia's hand. "I told James, somehow, we had to work things out."

Tavia buried her head in her hands. "I feel terrible about Jewel. She was so kind to me. If it weren't for her, Adam would have passed me by that day. She's the one who made him stop. I wish you could have known her."

"I do, too." Annie plucked a tissue from the box on the table and dabbed it at her eyes. "I knew if Adam loved her she had to be a beautiful person. How sad it is that the two of them were deprived of a life together. They had so many plans."

James nodded. "Adam would have made a fine doctor. He had a real compassionate heart. His patients would have loved him."

"Jewel would have made a wonderful wife for him," Tavia told them, smiling through her tears. "She loved him so. You could see it written on her face each time she looked at him."

"Adam said Jewel and I were very much alike." Annie's fingers rotated at her temples. "What a tragedy. It makes me sick to think that beautiful girl has been out in that canyon all this time, and no one found her."

"One thing really worried us," James said, turning toward Tavia. "We were afraid when Jewel's body was discovered you might be found and arrested, even though we weren't pressing charges." He leaned forward, his elbows resting on his knees. "I talked to a lawyer friend of mine, and since Jewel had no family to file charges against you for not reporting her missing when you were finally able to talk, and we don't plan to file any, and he doubted anyone else would, he thought there was a good possibility, after a hearing, the whole thing would be dropped."

Tavia's eyes widened at his words. "He said that?"

"Well, a judge might require you to do some public service of some kind, but my friend said even that was unlikely since no charges were being filed against you."

"I'd already planned to do that. Maybe, in Jewel's name, I can volunteer at the hospital, or help at a food kitchen, read to the blind, work at the rescue mission. I don't know exactly what but I feel I have to do something to make this world a better place."

Tavia was still in a state of shock. "So let me get this straight—all four of you can forgive me? Really forgive me? After the trouble I've caused?"

With smiles of reassurance, the four of them nodded.

"I have to know." Tavia swallowed hard and turned to face Annie and James, the words sticking in her throat. "Did you find Jewel?"

James nodded. "Her body had washed downstream in the spring rains. We gave her a beautiful graveside service performed by our pastor. Jewel is finally at rest with her Lord and with Adam."

Tavia's heart was so deeply touched, she could barely speak. She'd wanted that so much for the lovely young woman who had befriended her. "Thank you. I can't tell you how important that was to me. Jewel was a very special person. I wish I could have known her better. I'm going to spend the rest of my life trying to make things up to her, and to you."

"Beck loves you, Tavia," Annie said as she gestured toward Beck, tears filling her eyes once more. "He's a good man."

Beck shyly slipped an arm about Tavia's waist. "If I have my way, we'll be together for a long time. There's so much I want to know about you." He cupped her chin with his free hand and lifted her face toward his. "I'm not a wealthy man. I'll never be able to give you a fine house like this one, but I have a goal. Someday, I plan to own that little fleet of trucks I was telling you about. But until that day, all I can offer you is the life of a truck driver's wife. I'm on the road most of the week, and while it's not the most comfortable thing to do and can get pretty boring at times, if you'll consent to be my wife, I'd like for you to ride along with me as often as you can. I want you by my side—" He paused with a grin. "Not in the back seat. We'll see the country together."

Tavia was all smiles. "You mean it? You really want to marry me?"

James cleared his throat loudly. "Hey, I'd like to say a few words about this arrangement."

"Number one. You have to allow Annie and me to give you the church wedding we wanted to give Adam and Jewel."

"Number two," Annie said, smiling happily at the pair. "James and I want to be grandma and grandpa to any children you two might have. Remember, those children and I will have the same blood flowing through our veins."

"Enough talk, Annie. I think this young couple would like a few minutes alone." James reached out his hand to his wife. "And I'd like some time alone with my wife, the love of my life."

"It's time," James told Tavia a month later as they stood in the bride's room at their church, listening as the organ began to play.

Annie made one last adjustment to Tavia's veil then stood back to admire her. "You're the loveliest bride I've ever seen. I am so proud of you. You're as beautiful in that dress as I knew you'd be."

Tavia fought back tears, sure they would ruin her makeup and she'd end up with raccoon eyes. "You two are the sweetest people in the world. God has been so good to me, Annie. I can't thank you and James and Grandpa enough for all you have done."

Annie fastened the gold chain with the tiny baby ring about Tavia's neck. "Are you sure you want to wear this? You don't have to, you know."

"Oh, yes, I want to wear it. It's my something old. And this way Adam and Jewel are here with us." Fingering it lovingly, Tavia smiled, then gently planted a kiss on Annie's cheek. "I love you, Annie. I—I never meant to hurt you. You have to know that."

"I love you, too, and I don't want to hear another word about the past." Annie smiled through her tears. "Now, go, my darling daughter. Beck is waiting for you."

"And who gives this woman to be married to this man?"

Both Annie and James smiled at Tavia and then answered in unison, "We do."

Tavia turned and fondly placed a kiss on each one's cheek. "Without you, none of this would be possible."

She listened closely to each word as the pastor spoke, occasionally taking a peek at the handsome groom standing at her side holding on to her hand. Surely, any moment she'd wake up and this glorious moment would evaporate into nothingness.

"I now pronounce you husband and wife," the pastor was saying. "What God hath joined together, let no man put asunder." Then smiling and gesturing toward Beck, he added, "You may kiss your bride."

Slowly, as if he wanted to make the moment last forever, Beck turned Tavia to face him and gazed lovingly into her eyes. Lifting the veil from her face, he lowered his mouth onto hers, holding her captive with his love.

When their kiss ended and Beck finally released her, the pastor held his palm above their heads. "Go in peace. Love God and love one another, and may you have a blessed marriage, Mr. and Mrs. Beck Brewster."

The church filled with music as the newly married

couple hurried down the aisle, holding hands and smiling at all their new friends.

"We did it!" Beck scooped Tavia up in his arms and spun her around as soon as they reached the foyer. "We're married, Tavia! We're actually married!"

She slipped her arms about his neck and smiled up into his handsome face, her heart filled with wonder. Never had she been this happy.

Beck kissed the tip of her finger. "I'll be there for you, sweetheart. I'll never leave you. That's a promise."

Tavia lifted her face to his, gently brushing his lips with hers. *Thank you, God.*

Epilogue

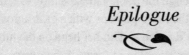

Three years later

"This motel isn't too bad. At least it's clean. We've stayed in a whole lot worse, and we've stayed in a whole lot better during the past three years I've been traveling with you," Tavia told Beck as she pulled something from a small sack of things they'd purchased at the discount house when they'd pulled into Cheyenne with a load, and slipped it into her pocket. "As long as I'm with you, any motel is fine."

"I'd give you the moon if I could, you know."

Tavia wrapped her arms about Beck's neck and twined her fingers through his hair. "I know, and I love you for it, but the only thing I want out of life is to love you and be the woman God would have me be." She pushed away from him and headed for the bathroom. "I want to freshen up a bit. It's been a long day."

Beck watched her go. How could he love someone as much as he loved her? Tavia was everything he'd ever wanted in a wife, and more. So much more.

Suddenly, a loud scream came from the bathroom.

Beck rushed through the door, half expecting to find Tavia sprawled on the floor, perhaps with a gash across her head where she'd fallen and hit her head on the tub. But instead, she was standing in front of the mirror, a silly grin across her face and she was crying.

"What? What's wrong? Are you sick? Are you hurt?" Beck was beside himself with worry.

Tavia's palms cupped his face and she kissed him hard on the mouth, her excitement overwhelming. "What is the best news I could tell you?"

He struck a thoughtful pose. "You won the lottery?"

She slapped at him playfully. "No, you silly, you know I don't buy lottery tickets."

"You're gonna get a job so I can retire?"

Again, she swatted at him. "You're going to be a daddy! See! Look at the little tester. Oh, Beck, we're finally going to have a baby!"

Beck pushed past her and sat down on the bed, staring off into space, repeating over and over, "I'm going to be a daddy. I'm going to be a daddy. I'm going to be a daddy!"

He pulled Tavia onto the bed beside him and began

to fuss over her. "Shouldn't you be resting? Are you taking enough vitamins? Don't you need to see a doctor right away? Have you been drinking enough water?"

"I'm fine, Beck. Having a baby is a perfectly normal thing. Calm down. Don't be such an old worrier."

He slipped his arm about her shoulders and cuddled her close. "This is great news. Me, a daddy. I can't believe it."

"You're going to be a wonderful father. Maybe even better than James."

He shook his head. "That man is a hard act to follow, but I'm going to do my best." He stroked her hand, then lifted her palm to his lips and kissed it. "You're going to make a beautiful mother."

She stood up quickly. "We have to call Annie and James!"

Beck nodded, picked up the phone and dialed in his phone card number, then the number for the Flints' home. Annie answered on the first ring.

Holding the phone between them, Beck and Tavia shouted out, "You're going to be grandparents!"

"Grandparents? Oh, wait! I have to tell James and Grandpa." They could hear some kind of discussion going on in the background, then Annie's voice again. "James is as excited as I am, but Grandpa said to tell you he's much too young to be a great-grandfather."

She and Beck laughed. "Tell him there's nothing he can do about it now. It's a done deal! Our baby is on the way."

"I'll tell him, No—wait! Grandpa says he wants to talk to you. Hold on."

"Hey, you two lovebirds, this is Grandpa. You'd better hurry home. You have another wedding to plan."

Covering the phone with her hand, Tavia looked quickly at Beck. "Who could he be talking about? We don't know anyone who is getting married, do we?"

He shrugged. "Beats me. I can't think of anyone."

Tavia uncovered the phone. "Beck and I can't think of anyone we know who is even engaged. Who's getting married, Grandpa?"

With a jubilant laugh, Grandpa replied, "Me!"

* * * * *

Dear Reader,

Hello! Let me introduce myself. My name is
Joyce Livingston and it has been my pleasure to write
this book, *The Heart's Choice*, for Love Inspired.

The Heart's Choice is the story of Tavia MacRae and
Beck Brewster, two lonely people who are thrown together
in the most unlikely of circumstances. Sometimes, life
throw us a curve, and it certainly threw one at Tavia and
Beck. What happened to them could happen to any of us
at any time. Has life ever thrown you a curve? How did
you handle it? Did you turn the reins of your life over to
God, or did you muddle on through yourself, running into
one insurmountable obstacle after another? I hope you
enjoy reading how Tavia and Beck responded when their
world fell apart.

Although I have had a number of inspirational romance
books published, this is my very first book for Love
Inspired. Writing inspirational romance for you, the
reader of Love Inspired, is a dream come true. A number
of years ago, God called me to be an encourager to women
everywhere, but I never dreamed it would be through my
writing. Yet, He has given me this wonderful opportunity,
and I praise Him for it.

I'd love to hear your comments about *The Heart's Choice*.
If you'd be willing to pray for me as I write these books,
I invite you to become a part of my prayer team. E-mail
me at: joyce@joycelivingston.com, or visit my Web site
at www.joycelivingston.com.

Till next time,

Joyce Livingston

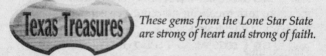

Take 2 inspirational love stories FREE!

PLUS get a FREE surprise gift!

Mail to Steeple Hill Reader Service™

In U.S.
3010 Walden Ave.
P.O. Box 1867
Buffalo, NY 14240-1867

In Canada
P.O. Box 609
Fort Erie, Ontario
L2A 5X3

YES! Please send me 2 free Love Inspired® novels and my free surprise gift. After receiving them, if I don't wish to receive anymore, I can return the shipping statement marked cancel. If I don't cancel, I will receive 4 brand-new novels every month, before they're available in stores! Bill me at the low price of $4.24 each in the U.S. and $4.74 each in Canada, plus 25¢ shipping and handling and applicable sales tax, if any*. That's the complete price and a savings of over 10% off the cover prices—quite a bargain! I understand that accepting the books and gift places me under no obligation ever to buy any books. I can always return a shipment and cancel at any time. Even if I never buy another book from Steeple Hill, the 2 free books and the surprise gift are mine to keep forever.

113 IDN DZ9M
313 IDN DZ9N

_____
Name   (PLEASE PRINT)

_____
Address   Apt. No.

_____
City   State/Prov.   Zip/Postal Code

Not valid to current Love Inspired® subscribers.

Want to try two free books from another series?
Call 1-800-873-8635 or visit www.morefreebooks.com.

* Terms and prices are subject to change without notice. Sales tax applicable in New York. Canadian residents will be charged applicable provincial taxes and GST. All orders subject to approval. Offer limited to one per household.

® are registered trademarks owned and used by the trademark owner and or its licensee.

INTLI04R   ©2004 Steeple Hill

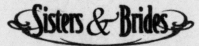